A
Harlequin
Romance

OTHER
Harlequin Romances
by DOROTHY CORK

Many of these titles are available at your local bookseller,
or through the Harlequin Reader Service.

For a free catalogue listing all available Harlequin Romances,
send your name and address to:

HARLEQUIN READER SERVICE,
M.P.O. Box 707, Niagara Falls, N.Y. 14302
Canadian address: Stratford, Ontario, Canada.

or use order coupon at back of book.

THE GIRL AT SALTBUSH FLAT

by

DOROTHY CORK

HARLEQUIN BOOKS   TORONTO
WINNIPEG

Original hard cover edition published in 1973
by Mills & Boon Limited.

© Dorothy Cork 1973

SBN 373-01757-X

Harlequin edition published February 1974

*All the characters in this book have no existence outside the
imagination of the Author, and have no relation whatsoever to
anyone bearing the same name or names. They are not even
distantly inspired by any individual known or unknown to the
Author, and all the incidents are pure invention.*

The Harlequin trade mark, consisting of the word
HARLEQUIN and the portrayal of a Harlequin, is registered
in the United States Patent Office and in the Canada Trade
Marks Office.

Printed in Canada

1757

CHAPTER ONE

'WELL,' thought Christine Vance as she stepped out into the sunshine of the Adelaide street and flipped her red hair behind her ears, 'that's an end to that.'

Her clear grey eyes were troubled and at first she did not see the man who was waiting on the pavement for her, smoking a cigarette. Tall, broad-shouldered, well dressed, his hair thick and light brown with sun-bleached streaks in it; his eyes the soft blue of hyacinths, though the square cleft chin and the deeply bronzed skin made one look twice to make sure that such a blue could belong to a face so strongly masculine and dynamic. He tossed his cigarette on the pavement and ground it out with the heel of a shoe of beautifully polished brown leather. His eyebrows peaked up quizzically, wrinkling his forehead as Christine caught his enquiring glance.

'Hello, Burton. Fancy seeing you.' She didn't smile, she wasn't in the mood for it, and he had to catch at her arm as she made to swing past him, her face averted.

'It didn't go well? Then I'm sorry—but don't take it out on me. Come and have some lunch and we'll talk it over.'

'There's nothing to talk over,' said Christine, trying to make nothing of her disappointment. To have been knocked back so swiftly and positively the first time she had ever applied for a position! She had lost the little confidence she had had when she came to the interview, but as yet hadn't reached the stage of wondering what came next.

Burton Alexander hailed a cab and despite herself she got into it.

'Melbourne Street.'

He settled himself beside her and although she turned

5

away from him and looked through the window, he persisted, 'No job? I rang your aunt and she told me you'd gone to see the employment agency.'

'Did she?' Chris was indifferent. She changed the subject. 'What are *you* doing in town? I thought you were going back to Red Sands after you fixed up buying that property you were after.'

'I did go back. But my business wasn't quite concluded and I had to make another trip. I thought I'd look you up and see what colour your world was.'

'It's grey,' said Chris flatly.

'Is losing out on a job the end of everything? Or is grey just—your colour?'

Chris didn't answer. She didn't like the way he said that. And it was the first time she had ever been aware of a positive lack of sympathy from him with her sore heart. Well, she wasn't much used to sympathy anyhow, so that was all right.

The taxi pulled up and Burton helped her out. She stood on the pavement while he paid the fare, a slim girl of twenty in a water-green cotton dress, with tan sandals and tan linen handbag, her red hair shining in the hot midday sunlight. The street was quaint, with its old bluestone houses restored and transformed into smart shops and restaurants and boutiques. This particular restaurant was shaded by a trellis covered with grapevines, it was painted white and called Douce France, and advertised French provincial cooking. Chris's heart was not too numb to feel an extra stab of pain.

Burton joined her, took her arm again, and eyed her narrowly as he asked, 'How do you feel about French cooking, Christine? I don't want to overburden you with memories and nostalgia, and let myself in for a watery noon.'

'Does he really expect me to cry?' she wondered. If she'd been almost any other girl, her eyes would have been brimming with tears of self-pity that anyone could be so callous about a hurt so real. But Chris was not by nature a girl who cried, and she had wept all her tears after her mother had

6

died and she had come home to find the man she loved—Francis Rogeon—engaged to her cousin Pam Gilcrist. She had wept for two solid days then, and the family had been scandalised at such excesses. Yet, after all, what else was to be expected of a daughter of Ashley Vance, who had been a rogue and had gambled away her mother's share in the great Gilcrist vineyards? And whose mother, let's face it, had proved herself the one weak member of the family—a wayward, silly girl, who had made a sorry mess of her life—a fact that had never been forgotten.

Chris had been hustled out of New South Wales as soon as she was deemed fit to travel, away from Millunga, her cousin Mitchell's vineyard, where Francis, a struggling young French vigneron, was a neighbour, and off to South Australia. There, one of the Gilcrist aunts was holidaying in the Adelaide hills, and the task of deciding what was to be done with Christine was designated to her.

The decision had finally been made. Chris was to go to secretarial school in Adelaide. A nice family would be found and she would be boarded out. Chris, though she was twenty, was not consulted. Perhaps she was thought incapable of making decisions, but she made one then. She was not going to secretarial school. She liked the bush, and rebelled at the thought of being incarcerated in the city—even a city as agreeable as Adelaide. All her life, except when she was away at boarding school, for as long as she could remember, had been spent at Mitchell's vineyard in the Hunter Valley, for it was Mitchell who had come to the rescue of her mother when her rascally husband had inconsiderately died of a heart attack and left her almost penniless with a small girl on her hands. Mitch had never made snide or unkind remarks or asides about Christine, and she had been truly grateful to him, despite a little mild schoolgirl rebellion about various of his edicts that she had thought too stern. But now *he* couldn't help her. Plainly, he could not have her around when Francis was going to marry his own sister, and when Francis's vineyard bordered on his own estate. And when Chris was so obviously shattered by it all. None of the other Gilcrists in the Riverina, where the big vineyards were, wanted her. She wasn't one of them. She was the outsider, the black sheep, the unknown quantity.

Well, Chris didn't want to go to them. But her heart was not in the city, and she snapped out of the state of apathy into which she had fallen since her world had toppled about her ears enough to look through the ads in the daily paper and apply for a position as governess-cum-mother's-help in the country.

That was today. And she hadn't even got past the woman at the employment agency.

'We couldn't possibly send you out, even on trial,' the poised, slightly supercilious woman at the agency had told her. 'You've no qualifications, no home background that could be a help, and, quite frankly, I don't think you have a very real interest in the position. So I'm sorry—no, and I'm afraid I have no alternative suggestions to make, except to advise you to try for a city job first, where you'll be close to home.'

It was like a game of snakes and ladders, and Chris was back to the starting point, and just now the fire had gone out of her. What was the use? Maybe she should just pack her things and get on a train for—anywhere!

'French cooking okay?' Burton Alexander persisted. They were inside the cool restaurant now, and the waitress was pulling out a solid dark chair from an equally solid and plain table by an open window that looked on to the grape arbour.

Chris sat down.

'I've never tasted French cooking.'

'Your Frenchman didn't cook?' He took the menu from the waitress and looked at Chris over the top of it with slightly mocking surprise.

'No,' said Chris.

'One thing less for you to regret, then. But there's nothing quite like French cooking. Shall I choose?'

'Yes,' said Chris. 'But I'm not hungry.'

'Pining in thought? Better watch it, or you'll be too thin for health—and beauty.' He ordered onion soup, beef Bourgignonne and salad, and asked for a carafe of red wine. The wine, more than anything else, reminded her piercingly of Francis, and she wondered if Burton realised it.

She had met Burton a month ago—soon after she came to Adelaide. Her cousin Richard had been dating a girl called Frith Alexander. She was a fashion artist, a tall girl, with silver-gilt hair that looked wonderful against her smooth tan. Frith's brother from the outback was in town on legal business and wanted to meet Richard, and Frith wanted another girl in the party. Richard suggested Chris who agreed for one reason only—her other two cousins were out and she couldn't face dinner alone with her aunt. And so she met Burton.

She was certain he had been told about her. Frith would have known through the Gilcrists of her love affair. 'Christine's cut up because she didn't come out the winner in the Francis Rogeon stakes.' They said things like that and they probably thought, 'What did she expect—competing against a *true* Gilcrist—and especially with parents like hers!' At any rate, when the evening was over he had kissed her goodnight—probably because most girls expected it. When she pulled away from him, he had said coolly, 'So it's still like that, is it? My apologies for rushing in.'

All the same, he had asked her to a concert the next day—'just for company'. And she went—'just to get out of the house'. He treated her casually, impersonally, and, relieved, she had thought he respected her grief. She saw him another two or three times, and once, after they had been to a Beethoven concert, her Aunt Patricia had warned her with a patronising smile, 'Don't pay too much attention to your little cultural outings with Burton Alexander, will you, Christine? He's a little sorry for you, I think. But he has the whole of the outback and the cities besides to choose from when he looks for a wife.' Chris had swallowed hard and bitten back a retort. She wasn't interested in a love affair, and Burton knew it. He knew her heart was sore, for

9

by then she had actually spoken to him of Francis, finding it a relief to talk to someone unprejudiced. She thought of him as a chance acquaintance who would listen without being involved. She was as she was, and he wasn't interested in changing her. His cattle run, Red Sands, was way off in the outback, but business was keeping him in Adelaide for a week or two. She gathered he was negotiating to buy up some property that was for sale, and when he went back home—and that had happened some ten days ago—she hadn't expected to see him again.

Now he was here and she wasn't at all sure that she was pleased to see him.

The onion soup came, and he said thoughtfully, 'So you've decided what to do with yourself, have you, Christine?' He buttered a piece of crisp roll and gave her a considering look.

'What do you mean?' Chris refused rolls and tasted her soup. It was as delicious as it smelt, and she was aware that she was more than a little hungry after all.

'What do I mean? For God's sake, haven't you just been chasing after some job, all eagerness—all full of life? That's what I heard from your aunt.'

Well, she had pretended eagerness to her aunt. But she told Burton candidly, 'They want to send me to secretarial college—to board me out with a *nice* family in the city. So I thought I'd try for a job in the bush. It wasn't much—a sort of mother's help thing, but'—she shrugged—'the agent didn't like me. I almost thought Aunt Pat must have been on the phone warning her off.'

'You did?' His oddly blue eyes regarded her none too kindly. 'I rather think you have a bit of a complex about your relatives, Christine. They seem to be a reasonably kind-hearted lot, and they've certainly been pretty good to you. I shouldn't object in the least to Frith's tying up with them. As for you—a moody girl in the process of recovering from a schoolgirl crush can be very wearing on the patience, you know.'

A schoolgirl crush! Chris's eyes pricked. She felt upset

10

by Burton's needling.

'It was not a schoolgirl crush,' she said. 'And I certainly don't want to be on their hands for ever.'

'Well then, what *do* you want? Let's hear all about it, I'm interested. But eat up your soup, for God's sake. Haven't you been starving yourself for love long enough?'

Christine put down her soup spoon. She said furiously, 'I told you I wasn't hungry. And I'm not going to eat just because someone tells me to. You're as bad as my relations, trying to push me around. I'm not sick and I'm not a child.'

'You're not a child, but you're certainly sick. We both know that even if we haven't discussed it ... Don't eat, then. But excuse me, I have a good appetite and a frame that requires a good few calories. Meanwhile, let's hear your views on your future career.'

'I haven't any,' said Chris unco-operatively.

He looked at her straight and square, and he wasn't in the least impersonal now, he was definitely critical. Chris didn't much like it. She looked down at her hands, not answering him. They were good hands, long and narrow with fingers that were slightly square at the tips. Once they had helped Francis—to tie his vines, to prune them, to cut the bunches of grapes during vintage. They had even, on occasion, swept and dusted his house for him, and they had been clasped more times than she could remember around his neck while he kissed her. For close on two and a half years she had dreamed of marrying Francis—of being Christine Rogeon. Without those dreams she felt quite lost. It had been because of Francis, and because of her ailing mother, that she had never given a thought to a career.

She looked up, and Burton was waiting for her to answer. She said slowly, 'I never wanted a career. I only wanted Francis.'

She saw his expression harden. 'Well, that appears to be one thing you can't have, doesn't it?'

Her temper flared again—the hot temper she had learned to discipline during the long months of her mother's final illness. 'I don't know about that. Maybe I could have

11

Francis yet. I was dragged off here before I was ready to fight. I could go back to the Valley and ask Francis why—why——' Her voice grew jagged, cracked, and she broke off, biting hard on her lip.

'Why he didn't choose you?' Burton had pushed aside his soup bowl, and the waitress brought the beef and the salad. Chris allowed Burton to put a portion on her plate but swore to herself that she would barely nibble at it. He said practically, as he served himself, 'Don't do *that*, Christine. You'd only make a fool of yourself. You wouldn't win any tricks at all.'

'How do you know?'

'Well, look at it this way: What could *you* do for Francis? Marriage is mainly, when you get down to facts, an economic contract. The French see it that way—they're realists. If this young vigneron needs money to build up his vineyards and his machinery and so on, then he's doing a prudent and far-sighted thing in marrying a girl who's well cashed up. You're not cashed up, are you, Christine? I believe your father saw to that.'

She winced a little at his brutality, but it was the brutality of what he said about Francis rather than what he said about her father.

'So how could you help him, Christine? Maybe he'd have liked you in his bed, and gracing his home, when you grew up a bit. You're a pretty girl, an attractive girl, to those who fancy redheads. But this cousin of yours, Pam, she has something more than looks to offer. Maybe he even loves her,' he said thoughtfully, without so much as a glance at Chris—he was more interested in his food. 'Maybe she's even prettier than you. From what I've seen of them, the Gilcrists don't lack for looks ... So all things considered, I'd say that haring off back to the Valley is definitely out, and you'd better forget it. Any ideas beyond that—now that today's effort has produced a blank?'

'No,' said Chris flatly. She had the curious feeling that Burton, of whom she had never really expected anything at all, had let her down. She wondered if his business affairs had turned sour on him, and put him out of humour. She hated him for saying things that she had never allowed herself to think. Not only about Pam's money, but the fact that Francis could actually love her. Pam was pretty—very pretty. She was intelligent too, and generous, and she had plenty to be generous with. But Chris had been so sure *she* was the one Francis loved.

'Your main need right now,' said Burton presently, having dispatched with enjoyment the best part of his meal, 'is to avoid the secretarial school and the nice family. Agreed?' He raised his blue eyes and looked across at her with an oddly frank air, and Chris said, 'Yes. I hate the city.'

'Well then.' He laid down his fork and leaned towards her with a smile. 'How about this, Christine—how about becoming temporarily engaged to me and coming out to Red Sands for a while? That's the bush if you like—the never-never, the great outback.'

Chris stared at him astonished. Was this a joke? Or could he possibly mean it?

'You mean,' she said after a moment of stunned thought, 'not really engaged at all?'

'For heaven's sake—what do you think?' His brows tilted, and his mouth, that had a suddenly discovered dimple at one corner, twisted in a sardonic grin.

Chris was still at a loss. She looked at him warily. Did he think that her father's daughter would grab at just any straw? And in any case, what was his idea? She said, somewhat inadequately, 'It's hardly a *job* you're offering me.'

His eyes were determined. He shoved his plate away and wiped his mouth on his table napkin. The waitress, hovering near with a question about coffee, withdrew.

'I didn't say it was. There'd certainly be no pay attached. All I meant was—I'll shelter you until you've come to terms with yourself. It's painfully obvious you haven't yet. I'll save you the secretarial bit and the nice family and the futile chasing after dead-end mother's-help positions.'

'Thank you,' said Catherine—coldly, politely. 'But I couldn't possbily be engaged to you even temporarily. And

I don't see why you should suggest it.'

He leaned back, made some minute gesture that brought two cups of coffee instantly, pushed the sugar towards Christine and helped himself lavishly to cream.

'It occurred to me,' he said finally, 'because it would suit me very well to be engaged at this particular point in time. There's been a minor hurricane in a metaphorical sense in my part of the world lately. However, if you won't take it on, okay.'

Chris felt curious despite herself, and now she could not catch his eye. She asked reluctantly, 'Why would it suit you? I don't understand.' She sipped her coffee and he his, and she looked at him through a faint vapour of steam.

'Would you believe it,' he said with a wry smile, 'there's a girl on my tail. Let's just leave it at that.'

Chris stared at him. A girl on his tail. Aunt Patricia had said he had the whole of the outback and the cities as well to choose from if he wanted a wife. And she had an idea that Red Sands was one of those incredibly enormous cattle stations way out in the north-east corner of the state. She had never given it more than a glancing thought before, but she must have heard Aunt Pat or Richard talking about it. After all, Richard was in love with Burton's sister, though Frith did seem to have dropped out of the conversation somewhat lately now she came to think of it. So, Chris thought, a girl on his tail must surely be nothing new. This one must be very hard to shake off if the production of a flesh and blood fiancée was necessary to accomplish the deed! She tried to imagine herself acting as Burton Alexander's fiancée and failed utterly. He was years older than Francis—far too worldly and mature for her. And if she couldn't fool herself, then she would never be able to fool anyone else. She wasn't good at pretending. She shook her head.

'I'm sorry. I could never do it.'

'No? Forget it then.' He pushed back his chair impatiently and stood up, waited for her to go ahead of him out of the restaurant and joined her a moment later under the

14

grape arbour outside, where she stood staring at the sunny street with a peculiar feeling of loss and blankness. They began to walk and she didn't ask where. She felt uneasy, ungrateful, and even churlish. How could he make her feel like that? After a moment she said, as though continuing a conversation, 'It's a ridiculous thing to ask. I couldn't possibly pretend to be engaged——'

'You could if you weren't so determined to stick to your sticky schoolgirl past—if you'd keep your sense of humour and your feet on the ground——'

Chris said angrily, 'I'm not a schoolgirl. And love must be something you just don't understand. When you're in love, you can't *help* yourself——'

They walked another ten yards in silence. Then Burton said, 'You're very young, Christine. Nineteen?'

'Twenty,' she flung out.

'I know how you feel. I remember being as young as that—fifteen years ago ... Well, listen to me, you can still come to Red Sands. I'll shelter you without exacting a price. Let's say I'm prepared to do it out of the kindness of my heart.'

'You don't have to bother with me.'

'Don't worry, you won't bother me out there,' he said dryly. 'Red Sands is a mighty big run—we needn't even see one another from one week's end to the next. It's an ideal place for the licking of wounds—a place to hide, to forget, and to be forgotten, if that's what you want. You might even learn to grow up there. It's not just the bush, but the harsh outback—not cosy and full of togetherness like your pretty little vineyard in the valley.'

Chris gave a bleak laugh. 'I think you're trying to put me off now.'

'Do I need to? I don't seem to have got you interested.'

She didn't look at him. Something about the idea of going to Red Sands appealed to her—it was so remote, so different. She said carefully, 'It would be one way of getting out of the family's hair.'

'It would at that. Exactly what I thought.' He stopped

15

walking and looked down at her seriously. 'Loneliness, vastness—just what a girl like you needs.'

'Yes,' said Chris soberly.

'Then you're invited. No strings, and no payment. Like to think it over? I'll call you tonight. I've got to get back tomorrow.'

With a feeling of reluctance, Chris agreed. She felt absurdly mean, as if she were asking for something for nothing. But it was a somehow enticing means of escape, and one that she couldn't help considering.

'If only,' she chided herself, 'there were something I really wanted to do. Like training to be a teacher or a nurse or something.' But all she wanted was—vaguely—the bush.

She felt oddly flat when they parted and she went home and told her aunt, 'I tried for a job, but I didn't get it.'

Her aunt looked at her curiously. 'I'm sorry if it was something that particularly appealed to you, Christine. But never mind, I've already made enquiries and I can enroll you at a very nice secretarial college, and I've heard of an elderly widow who'd like to take a paying guest. It won't be a great expense, and once you've completed the course you'll be quite independent.'

'You *hope*,' thought Christine bitterly. 'Meanwhile I'll be costing you money and I shan't be allowed to forget it.' If she had really thought, she'd have realised it would probably be Mitchell who would pay her fees and provide her with a living allowance, and he wouldn't make a song and dance about it, but would do it gladly. But just now it was anathema to think of the relatives handing out charity to her...

She had flung herself down in an armchair in the sitting room near a window that looked down the hills through lovely glades of trees. She said suddenly, dreamily, 'Never mind, Aunt Patricia. I shan't cost you another penny. I've fixed up something else for myself.'

'Have you?' Her aunt was working on some petit point, and she raised her head and looked at Chris sharply through the top lens of her bifocals.

Chris stretched out her shapely legs and put the long fingers of her two hands together and squinted at them.

'Yes. I'm going to the outback. Burton Alexander has asked me.'

She saw her aunt's jaw drop slightly, and she wanted to laugh. It was the first thing that had tickled her sense of humour in weeks.

'Burton has? You—you saw him, then? But—exactly what are you talking about, Christine? What do you mean?'

'I've an invitation to go and stay at Red Sands,' said Chris, her grey eyes innocent.

Her aunt frowned. 'I don't really think you should go, Christine. It's time for you to face the future. You must begin seriously to think in terms of—of some sort of career, a position——'

Chris stared at her hands, considering. What sort of a position could she fill at Red Sands? Could I be a cook, she wondered, a cowgirl? She looked up, her eyes bright and defiant. 'But I want to go, Aunt. I like the bush.'

Aunt Patricia pressed her lips together. 'Exactly what are you up to, Christine? Did you ask Burton Alexander if you might visit Red Sands? I shouldn't like to think you were taking advantage of the fact that Richard is friendly with Frith. It's not at all the right thing to do.'

Chris's eyes sparked. 'But then I don't have the reputation of doing the right thing, do I, Aunt?'

'No, I'm afraid you don't, Christine. You've been spoiled at Millunga—given everything—allowed to think you have only to ask and your every wish would be granted.'

'Well, I didn't have to ask this time,' Chris said with an air of triumph. Her aunt's criticism irked her. 'It was all Burton's idea. And—and he's asked me to marry him.'

Her aunt looked as if she had suddenly completely lost her bearings. She looked quite staggered.

'Well, what a surprise, Christine! I must admit I had no idea anything of the sort was in the air. Of course I'm delighted. Is it quite—official?'

17

Chris's heart plummeted. What on earth had she let herself in for? She wished she had kept quiet, but somehow it had been irresistible to stun her aunt like that. In fact, of course, Burton Alexander hadn't asked her to marry him at all. He had asked her to become temporarily engaged to him—as a favour. And she had refused. She looked down at her feet in their pretty tan sandals and said uneasily, 'I haven't really given him my answer yet.'

'Then you're a foolish girl. Such an opportunity! Are you afraid you won't like Red Sands? And even if people say you've been caught on the rebound, they'll envy you. Isn't that something—to a girl like you?'

Chris felt a spasm of pain and bit her lip. Her aunt was staring at her, assessing her, plainly wondering what on earth a man like Burton Alexander could see in a girl like Christine Vance. She said, her head up, 'I'm lucky, aren't I? A girl like me—with nothing of my own. But Burton doesn't need to make a marriage that's a—a sound economic contract. He has all the worldly goods one man could possibly need——'

Her aunt looked vaguely uncomfortable, and some devil made Chris continue. 'Some men actually like redheads. I will grace his home, he may even like me——' She stopped, confused, sickened by herself. 'In his bed,' she had been going to say. And at that instant the telephone rang.

Her aunt took the call, and in a minute Chris realised it was Burton.

'Burton? Christine has told us the news. We're very, very pleased, believe me.' Her voice was high-pitched and bright with excitement, and Chris writhed. She hurried to the telephone, feeling agonised. What must Burton think? What on earth was he saying? Whatever it was, her aunt smiled and said, 'Of course! She's here now, Burton.'

Burton said, sounding amused, 'Christine, you've surprised me. So it's to be a reciprocal arrangement, is it? Can I conclude that on second thoughts you've decided the strings weren't so disagreeable?'

'No, it wasn't like that,' said Chris guardedly.

18

'I'm disappointed. As a matter of fact, I'd thought up a tentative plan. I was going to suggest you come out on the 'Ghan in a day or two if you felt like it. But under the circumstances—seeing that we're—engaged'—his voice was dry—'it might be a better idea for you to fly home with me tomorrow. Can you make it?'

Chris could have backed out. She realised that later. But weakly she gave in—to fate. After all, Red Sands was a big cattle run, and as well, she was aware of an immense inner relief. A decision had been made, she was about to break away from the Gilcrist family and start on her own. They had, Burton had insisted, been kind to her. In their way, she qualified that, and maybe she was inordinately sensitive, but she knew they would be glad to have her unloaded on to someone else. How surprised they would all be to find it was on to someone like Burton Alexander! They would not be nearly so surprised when the engagement came to an end, but by that time she would have decided on some new course for herself.

All this flashed rapidly through Christine's mind as she half listened to Burton's instructions, not only as to when he would pick her up, but also as to what she had better bring with her in the way of clothing.

'And if you don't have riding clothes,' he was saying, 'we'll get you some before we leave Adelaide.'

'I always wear jeans when I ride,' said Christine. Riding made her think of evenings with Francis when they had taken horses and cantered about on the green hillside up above the long rows of grapevines, while the soft air of the valley caressed them invisibly, and later Francis kissed her in the last of the golden sunlight...

It was Burton who kissed her the next day when he came in a cab to collect her. He had flown down from the north in his own small aircraft and he would take Chris back in it. Aunt Patricia was still too surprised to entirely believe what had happened. But after all, the Gilcrists were people of standing, and Chris was half a Gilcrist. She tried to conceal her delight at being rid of Christine in her delight

19

at the news.

'We had no idea! Of course you want to take her back to Red Sands to see how she likes the country life. I'm sure she will. You're used to the country, aren't you, Christine?'

'Yes,' said Chris. She was watching Burton warily, but not by the movement of a muscle did he reveal that this was anything but a genuine engagement. He said, smiling down at her aunt, 'I certainly hope she'll like the outback, Mrs Gilchrist. It's a little different from the Valley—and from the Riverina! But here's hoping.' And then, when she was least expecting it, he reached out and drew her to him with a forcefulness that was unexpected and impossible to combat. 'We haven't cemented our pact in the usual way yet, have we, Chris?' he said, and kissed her lingeringly on the lips.

Chris was affronted and shocked. She shrank from him, but he held her relentlessly, and her aunt at least was apparently thoroughly convinced by their embrace.

An hour or so later, as she sat beside him in his small aircraft looking down at the tiny receding city of Adelaide, Burton remarked conversationally, 'I hadn't realised before just how much on ice that heart of yours still is, Christine. Kissing you is like kissing an ice maiden. Definitely chilling. Are you wishing you hadn't said you'd be engaged to me? I gave you a choice, you know. You didn't have to play it this way. Why did you?'

Chris said wearily, 'Aunt Patricia goaded me. I guess I wanted to set her back by the ears.'

He looked at her narrowly and laughed, but not with much amusement. 'I see.'

He said nothing more and the subject wasn't mentioned again on the long journey north and still further north. In a way, Chris enjoyed the flight. She had only been up in a small plane once before, and that was when she was a child and Mitch had taken her up for a joyride. She had enjoyed it then, and she was enjoying it today—with reservations.

Late in the afternoon they flew over the glitter of saltpans, and Chris saw the occasional flash of a dam, vast floodplains spreading out around the dry watercourses, great boulders that made purple shadows on the gibber plain. And there was a strip of lush dark green where trees grew and water shone, incongruous against the reds and greys of the desert lands, the open plains and the sand-hills—a tiny strip from this high up, but from down on the ground no doubt immense. She knew they must soon reach Red Sands and she thought with a fainting of the spirit, 'What have I done?' True, she had escaped a life that had been uncomfortable to her, but now she faced with trepidation the notion of posing as someone's fiancée in a slice of country so underpopulated that everyone must know everyone else. She would never be able to do it!

Minutes later, the man beside her said bracingly, 'Well, we're almost home. Right on the edge of the sandhill country. Like it?' She glanced at him, and the light of sundown shone on his face so that it was warm, burnished, golden. The tips of his lashes glittered like gold and there was gold in the brown of his hair, and a proud look on his face as he glanced down at the red plains below, made redder by the sunset, and dotted with a fantastic kind of see-through vegetation—the mulga.

Chris said edgily, 'I don't know yet. But I'd like it better if I didn't have to play this silly game of pretence.'

'Sorry. It's too late to back out now. I've let my book-keeper in on the good news and everyone knows by now. We can hardly decently pretend to have broken it off on the way here. Besides which, it suits me too well. Try to look at it as a piece of fun, will you?'

'I can't see it that way,' said Chris shortly.

'Your bad luck, then. How long is it since that crack appeared in your heart, Christine? It must be a good six or seven weeks, mustn't it? Too long ago to continue nursing it along. Even a really deep wound has pretty well healed up in that time—if the patient is young and healthy. It's time to give that heart of yours an airing, my girl, and here's a good place to do it.'

'That's clever talk,' said Christine, 'but I'm afraid it doesn't mean much. And it's this—this thing about being engaged to you that's so hideously impossible.'

'Why so?' His eyebrows went up. 'Most girls love play-acting of that kind. And think how you'll be able to wallow in your family's sympathy and commiseration when *this* affair comes to an end! I'll guarantee you'll get a ton more sympathy than you want.'

Chris swallowed hard. She thought Burton unchivalrous not to allow her to change her mind, particularly when he had said she was free to come here without any strings attached. She wished she had had the sense to keep her mouth shut when Aunt Patricia had goaded her ...

The plane was coming down now. She could see the cluster of buildings that was Red Sands station, the shine of rooftops, the dark lines of trees, the square of green marking the horse paddock ... Then the aircraft touched down on the station strip, and bounced lightly across the hard red earth, finally coming to a gentle standstill. The whole of the great open plain, and the long low line of ranges in the distance was bathed in a clear red light, and against the vast cloudless sky a flock of birds wheeled and turned silently. Chris stood looking about her, half expecting a girl to materialise—to come riding out of the sunhaze in a cloud of golden dust, hair flying, back straight, well-dressed in riding pants and immaculate shirt. The girl on Burton's tail. But no rider appeared. Instead, a jeep came racing up, braked to a sudden standstill and disgorged a tall dark man who came to meet them.

Burton took a firm hold of Christine's arm. 'Hi, Dan. This is my book-keeper, Dan Spencer, Christine—the first person to hear the good news. Dan, meet my fiancée, Christine Vance. Isn't she a honey?'

The other man smiled. He had a lean tanned face and a wide mouth that looked wry despite the rather diffident smile. He wore cord trousers, a dark shirt with a scarf knotted at the neck, and stockmen's boots. There was a touch silver at his temples, though he looked no more than forty, and his eyes, grey and perpetually narrowed, were looking at Christine with something more than a welcoming smile in them. Chris thought they were astutely summing her up, even while he told her cordially, 'I hope you'll like it here, Christine. I guess you're anxious to look us over.'

'Yes,' said Chris uncomfortably. She looked at Burton to give her a guide line, but he had turned aside to heave her stuff and his own out of the plane. He said, with a grin over his shoulder, 'Oh, Christine will love it here, Dan. She's a country girl, aren't you, Chris?' He spun round and put one arm carelessly around her waist, and she made a conscious effort not to pull away. She walked close at his side as all three moved over to the dusty jeep. She was installed in the back while the two men sat in the front, and Dan said before they started off, 'That's great, Christine, that you're a country girl. I had an idea you were from Adelaide.' He sounded friendly now, and that was something, but Chris felt a fool when Burton said mockingly, 'She's from the Hunter Valley, Dan—better be honest with you, you'll soon wheedle the truth out of the girl, if I know you.' He changed the topic briskly. 'Has Paddy got those cattle well on the move?'

'Sure. Though I understand there's no great hurry.'

'There is a hurry. I want them off Saltbush Flat in double quick time and no nonsense. I'll get out there myself tomorrow and see if Paddy's fooling about. One impression I don't want to create is that that land's invaluable to me. I've all of Red Sands at my disposal, that's the story.'

Chris, alone in the back of the jeep, thought to herself that Burton Alexander was throwing his weight about somewhere. She had been in more ways than one relegated to the back seat, and that was a relief. She began to see Burton in a slightly different light. In the city, he had been so suave, so very much at home in his expensive good-looking clothes. In the plane, while he had removed his coat, he had kept on his tie and kept his link with the city. His shirt was white, his trousers charcoal grey, and he looked like a wealthy man whose hobby was flying. Now, he had become a different man. The joyride was over, they had come down out of the sky into a world that was a very real one. Burton was once again the owner of a considerable cattle station, and as for Chris herself—there was an uncomfortable time ahead for her if she was going to keep the silly half-promise she had made.

If? What was to stop her saying, 'I'm sorry, I can't do this for you after all, and I want to go home.' There was a catch there. Home was nowhere. Nevertheless, she could *say* it. She could say she had decided she wanted to learn typewriting after all. It would be up to Burton then to explain away his engagement, and to grapple alone with the girl on his tail or to find someone better qualified than Chris, and more willing, to help him get rid of her. If that was what he wanted to do. She need never see him again.

Of course it would be mean—even dishonest. And despite the family belief that nothing much could be expected of Christine, she had never been that ...

By the time they had made the short run to the homestead, she had decided that she was certainly coming to the bush here in the north-east corner of the state. It looked about as much like the Hunter Valley as Sturt's desert pea looked like an orchid. She decided that it *could* be interesting, that it *could* take her mind off Francis and the date she had circled in black on her calendar—the date of his marriage to Pam.

Dan Spencer reduced speed as he drove the jeep past the horse paddock where some fifty or so fine horses were grazing; past the stock tank, the great windmill with its huge steel water tank; past a scattering of buildings, some small yards where there were turkeys and pigs, fowls and geese, and then through wide gates towards the homestead garden. There was a white fence, a collection of trees dominated by a row of tall date palms, and then the homestead itself. They pulled up in a gravelled yard, and Chris got out, feeling suddenly weary and a little lost. She walked down a pathway shaded by feathery tamarisks and cedars whose small star-shaped mauve flowers had a haunting perfume;

24

past the date palms and a tall hedge of bamboo that gave protection from the winds that blew in across the great open red plains. The homestead was long and low and cream-washed, its vast shady verandah draped with mauve wisteria and sweet-scented yellow jasmine. The underside of the roof was insulated with green material, and a row of doors opened impressively all of its length. As she climbed the steps, with Burton no more than an inch behind her, a woman came through one of the doors and stood on the verandah with a smile of greeting.

She was a very plain woman with shrewd blue eyes that scrutinised Christine harder and more openly than Dan's had done. Again, Burton's arm was around Chris's narrow waist as he introduced her. This was his housekeeper, Mrs Perry, and giggling and staring from the end of the verandah was a little group of aboriginal girls, barefooted, wearing clean cotton dresses, their dark eyes shining, their mouths stretched in grins that varied from the shy to the cheeky. Chris was hardly aware of them. The thing she was more aware of was Burton's arm around her waist and her own inner shrinking. She wanted to say, 'Don't touch me—I'm not engaged to you—you're not Francis.'

He glanced down at her and she realised she had not been listening to what was being said. His eyes, of that odd almost violet blue, were penetrating. He said, 'I'll show Christine to her room, Mrs Perry. It's been a long journey for her, and an eventful couple of days. Come along, Chris.'

Hers was a big cool bedroom with a bed that looked huge—almost a double bed; with pink cotton curtains and a pink and white quilt; with light polished floorboards and a hand-made rug in cream and soft green and pink; with flowers on the dressing table—white star-faced everlastings made into a little bouquet and tied with pink satin ribbon. Chris looked around the room, half delighted, half scared, and then she looked at Burton, who looked back at her steadily, quizzically.

'Pink for a redhead. Mrs Perry didn't know. Never mind —you'll like it here, I'm sure. This big room all to yourself to hide in, a cane lounger outside the door where you can lie and think about your love life all day if you like. I shan't bother you, Christine. I've plenty to do right now. Any time you want, you can come out with me, of course, but maybe it would be putting too much of a strain on that sick heart of yours yet.'

Chris turned away. 'Maybe it would. But I wish you'd forget about the engagement bit——'

'I don't want to forget it. I've told you, it's useful to me at present, and as well, it could be a discipline for you. Engaged girls don't mope. But perhaps you don't want discipline. You're a bit of an exhibitionist in your own way, I think.'

So he had heard of her crying fit up there in the Valley. Chris said, her grey eyes stormy, 'Well, what else can you expect from a girl with parents like mine? You must have been told all about them—my father a swindler, my mother a weak girl who let her heart rule her head——'

'Come off it, Christine,' he said irritably. 'I've not the vaguest interest in a lot of gossip about your parents. I'm only concerned with you. I invited you here to help you, remember?'

'To help yourself,' retorted Christine. 'So you say.' She picked up her suitcase and tossed it on the bed. 'I'm sorry I said I'd come. Well, I'll stay until——'

'You'll stay until you're fit to go.'

'My heart?'

'And your head.' He turned swiftly and reached the door. 'Do you want to eat with the rest of us—it won't be a French menu to tear at your heartstrings, I'm pretty sure— or are you going to indulge yourself with a tray in your room?'

'Since you've suggested it,' said Chris, whose nerves were ragged, 'I'll have a tray in my room.'

'Not strong enough to put up with my loving glances?'

'I just don't like acting.'

'It's no wonder. You don't put on a very good show.'

'You chose me for this role. I didn't ask for it.'

'You accepted it. I didn't even twist your arm. But I may have to do just that if you don't improve your performance.'

Chris turned her back. 'For whom?' she thought angrily, as she heard him go. There was no other girl around that she could see.

She sat down unhappily on the side of the bed and wished that she had settled for joining the others at dinner. That way, she would at least find out who the others were. Maybe one of them was this girl who was supposedly the cause of all the strife.

CHAPTER TWO

SHE opened her suitcase and rooted around impatiently among her clothes and came up with a dress she had bought some time before her mother died. It was a coral-coloured dress of soft cotton that looked like silk, a dress for romantic summer evenings. She had worn it once for Francis when he had come to Millunga for dinner. She remembered that Francis had kissed her that night. But then he had always been kissing her; he was a very demonstrative young man. She would have to throw away all her clothes if she was going to be touchy about wearing them because they reminded her of Francis. At any rate, she didn't need reminding of Francis . . .

She found a bathroom two doors along, and looking down the hallway calculated that there must be about ten bedrooms in this house. She wondered how many of them were empty. The warm darkness had fallen and the house seemed to be throbbing faintly as if a heart beat in it. It was a curiously warm and friendly house, and not so terribly old. Chris had vaguely expected an old-fashioned homestead where everything was Victorian and outsize. But this house was reasonably up to date, sparkling and somehow lively.

When she came back to her room, she slipped into the pretty coral dress, noting that she had lost a little weight since last she had worn it. She put her feet into sand-coloured shoes, brushed back her shining red hair and caught it at the back with a coral chiffon scarf, dabbed perfume—Mitchell had given her that for her twentieth birthday—at her wrists and on the lobes of her ears, and, feeling much restored, found her way to the kitchen. It was a huge gleaming room that opened on to the back verandah, and at one end a small dark-haired boy of four or five was seated at a little low table eating his supper of boiled egg and bread and butter.

Mrs Perry looked round from the stove, and Chris said, 'I don't want that tray, Mrs Perry. I'll come out to dinner after all. Can I help?' How much like a fiancée she sounded!—almost as though one day she would be taking over the ordering of this kitchen. Mrs Perry seemed unsurprised.

'I'm glad you've perked up, Christine. Lots of people feel shelled out by the time they get here. It's the bigness and emptiness of it all—it frightens you a bit. You'll settle all right. But you go inside. Burton will be in the sitting room—you'll find him there. I've plenty of help in the kitchen. Come along tomorrow if you feel like it.'

Burton was alone in the sitting room. He had poured himself a drink, and the glass stood on a small table, the cut surface glittering in the lamplight. There was a modern upright piano at one end of the long airy room, and he had opened the lid and stood fingering the keys absently, softly. Chris recognised the tune and stood motionless in the doorway.

'How shall I my true love know from another one?'

'Shakespeare,' she thought, her lips soundlessly making the words. When he moved, she thought he was coming to fetch his drink, or had perhaps become aware of her, but he sat down on the piano stool and began to play melody and accompanying bass with a sure and sensitive touch. His hands looked so brown and hard, yet they made that heart-catching music, so softly, so thoughtfully. Chris moved slightly, he turned his head and his eyebrows went up cynically, and he began to sing directly to her, 'He is dead and gone, lady, he is dead and gone——'

He broke off, closed down the piano lid and came towards her with a casual, 'Now what can have made me think of that old song tonight, I wonder? And what brought you out of your hidey-hole so soon, Christine? May I pour you a drink and express the hope that you'll stay and dine with us?—particularly since you're looking so delightfully pretty.'

There was irony in his tone, and Chris said a cool, 'Thank you. I'd like a dry sherry, please, if you have it.'

'Of course. It shall be the palest lightest driest sherry you've ever had in all your life. Please sit down.'

Chris sat in a hard chintz-covered armchair. The night was warm and the hardness was cool and comfortable. Burton, who had crossed to a long polished cabinet, now brought her a small sherry glass containing the promised drink.

'Keep a stiff upper lip as you drink it, Christine. No brimming eyes as you recall all the pale dry sherries you've drunk with your vigneron in happier days than these.'

Christine felt herself tense. Of course the sherry had made her think instantly and achingly of Francis, and it was hurtful to hear this man refer so unsympathetically and knowledgeably to the fact. It had the effect, however, of causing a door to shut abruptly on her personal pain, as though she must hide it from both him and herself.

He sat opposite her, at one end of the couch, reached for his own drink, crossed one long leg over the other, and said thoughtfully, 'I learned quite something about you and your recent past before we first met, Christine. I was warned in advance that you were in a very fragile state and must be handled with tact and consideration or there'd likely be floods of tears and fragments of broken heart all over the place. I thought it a pity you'd been asked along to dinner, under those circumstances.'

Chris raised clear grey eyes that she knew were openly hostile and found herself confronted by a hard unrelenting scrutiny. She said coldly, though a pulse was hammering maddeningly at her temples, 'You must surely have been disappointed, Burton. I don't recall shedding a single tear that particular evening.'

He glanced at the amber liquid in his own glass consideringly. 'No, I don't believe you did.' The hyacinth eyes suddenly plunged once more into hers. 'In fact, I got the impression that your tears, like the rest of you, were frozen up. Funny, that—fire-red hair and the rest of you as cold as ice. Are you really so frozen up you have no feelings left, Christine?'

Christine stared back at him furiously. At that moment, she was full of feelings and they were far from tender ones. She didn't take kindly to these constant gibes and needling, and she hadn't *asked* to come here. She was about to say so when there was a diversion, as Dan Spencer came into the room. He sent Chris a slightly wary smile, refused Burton's gesture that indicated, 'Help yourself to a drink,' and told them, 'Dinner's ready. Mrs Perry would like us to come right in.'

Christine let out her tensely held breath and rose at the same time as Burton. She was telling herself that she'd have done better to stay on in Adelaide; that Burton, far from helping her to forget, seemed intent on reminding her constantly of Francis. Intent too on making her aware that he thought her a fool of a girl to have fallen in love and come to grief. She wondered, as she moved with the men towards the dining room, if his purpose in asking her to Red Sands was solely and completely to serve ends of his own, and if the service he was supposed to be performing for her, that of giving her asylum until she decided what she wanted to do with her life, was a mere side issue. She had thought it kind of him, at one stage. Now she was far from sure. In

30

any case, he was doing precious little to help her slip into the role of fiancée and could hardly expect her to put on a show all by herself.

But this girl on his tail—who was she? And where was she?

Chris certainly did not find out that night. At the dinner table, besides Burton, Mrs Perry and herself, there was only Dan Spencer, and Dan was there because his wife was, as Christine already knew, away. There was no talk of another girl, and, happily enough, Burton desisted from any further baiting and treated Christine in the kindest and friendliest way possible. Apparently while there were others about he was determined that the fiction of their engagement should be made as credible as possible.

His friendliness, however, did not extend as far as taking her out on the run with him, and she was relieved the next couple of mornings to find him already gone when she got up, leaving her free to do as she pleased.

Not altogether unexpectedly, she found life around the homestead quite diverting. She wandered about on her own, exploring without going far, getting the feel of this almost desert country that was so different from anything she had known before. It was burningly hot by nine o'clock, but it was a dry heat and she found she could tolerate it fairly well. She wore a minimum of clothing and always equipped herself out of doors with the shady hat that Burton had advised her to bring. Mrs Perry was friendly and helpful, telling her where the riding horses were if she wished to ride, where the waterhole was if she fancied a swim, where the small aboriginal children, who didn't yet go to school, could be found if she was interested in them.

'Burton wants a schoolteacher here on the property, but we haven't got one yet. Not enough children. It's a shame for them to have to go away, but of course they must have proper schooling.'

On her second afternoon, Chris took her hat and wandered through the garden, past the date palms. She walked the length of the long rectangle of gravel that lay in front of the oil and food stores, the work shop and garages, made her way past the aboriginals' quarters to a dry creek bed shaded by pink-berried pepper trees, where, in the sand, a swarm of dark-skinned little children played. Chris had never had much to do with aboriginal children, and she stood some distance off watching their idle play with thoughtful eyes.

They were like she was, she thought—caught between two worlds, uncertain of their future. But hers was an easier and simpler position than theirs, by far. Her worlds were divided by what seemed just now an endless and desolate stretch that she would never manage to cross, but in actuality, she told herself philosophically, she would be over the worst of it in a year or so. By then it surely wouldn't hurt so much that she had lost Francis ... But these children—their worlds were ages apart. They did not yet fit comfortably into the white man's world, yet their old heritage, their old ways, were no longer available to them. Once, these little boys she was watching would, with their older brothers who were away at school now, have gone out with their fathers, to learn to hunt and to track. The little girls would have gone with their mothers to dig for edible roots, or witchetty grubs, to gather fibres to make into dilly bags. Now they must learn the strange ways of the white man, and one of their problems was to find a niche to fit into in a world that was not theirs.

'They *really* have problems,' thought Chris, a little ashamed of her own misery and self-absorption. What had *she* to moan about? Presently, feeling thoughtful but not on her own account, she wandered back towards the horse yards, going the long way round. She was leaning on the rail when Dan came riding back from inspecting one of the bore pumps. He asked her cheerfully, 'Enjoy your day, Christine?'

'Yes,' said Chris. 'I haven't *done* anything, but I've looked around—and I've done some *thinking*——'

'That's the idea. Are you going to like it enough to marry and live here?' The seriousness of his tone and of his grey eyes disconcerted her, and she turned her head away as she answered evasively. 'I've always liked the country.'

He swung down from his horse and in a moment was standing beside her, watching a couple of lean dusty young aboriginals showing off as they rode around the horse paddock. He said almost casually, 'This is not just the country, Christine. This is the edge of the desert. It's different.'

She looked at him in surprise.

'Well, I know that, Dan.'

'Peg—that's my wife,' Dan said, leaning on the rail and taking the makings of a cigarette from the pocket of his khaki shirt, 'Peg is a country girl. *Your* sort of country. Right now, she's having a spell down south, in the Barossa Valley. Young Annabel, the baby, has been feeling the heat and needs a change. So Peg says,' he added dryly.

'It is certainly hot,' said Chris. That morning, she had seen the heat waves dancing, making a strange shimmering sea of the plain where the saltbush grew.

'Yes, it's hot,' agreed Dan. 'But Peg doesn't fancy coming back here ever again.'

Christine's eyes widened. She thought of the little boy she had seen in the kitchen her first night at Red Sands. He was Dan's little boy, Jason, and Mrs Perry looked after him most of the time. 'But Jason's here,' she exclaimed. 'Of course she'll come back.'

He shrugged. 'For how long? I kept Jason because I was afraid of losing the lot of them. This is a hard land to learn to love, Christine, and Peg has never learned.' He looked at her hard, his grey eyes kind but regretful, and she knew he was asking her if *she* could learn to love this land—warning her not to make a mistake—forgiving her if she rejected and went, before it was too late. She couldn't tell him the truth. That for her, it didn't matter. She was here only temporarily in any event. She told Dan almost gently, 'I expect your wife misses her friends, her family. It's different for me—I'm on my own. So you mustn't worry about me, Dan, please——'

'I worry about every woman who comes here,' he said

briefly. 'One thing you can be sure of—the Boss wants you to take a good hard look around for yourself before you start setting any wedding date.'

Chris, feeling embarrassed, made a murmured sound that could have implied anything, and Dan said after a moment, 'If you'd like to come out with me tomorrow you're welcome. The stores will be in and I'll be driving out to the mustering camp at Five Mile Swamp. Not a long day, but you'll see a bit of the shape of the land.'

'I'd like that,' said Christine honestly.

Dan narrowed his eyes. 'We've had to alter our usual schedule this year, as I don't doubt you know. That's why the Boss has been on the go so early these last couple of mornings. Otherwise, *he*'d take you out,'

'I guess he would, Dan,' Chris agreed, though she thought no such thing. The Boss didn't want to be lumbered with her company when there was no audience to play to!

'He said you needed a bit of coddling for a while. That you'd had a hard time the last few months while your mother was ill.'

'Yes,' said Chris inadequately. Cunning Burton! So he had explained his neglect of her that way. She liked Dan, and felt a shocking fraud, but she was grateful to him for bothering about her, seeing that Burton couldn't be bothered showing her the 'shape' of the land. The early hours wouldn't trouble her. The truth was, he didn't want to take her out. Moreover, it didn't matter a cent to him whether she hated the sandhill country or whether she never even saw it, but spent each and every day around the homestead, moping and fretting and crying over the past.

Probably he thought she did just that . . .

She went out with Dan the following day in one of the station jeeps which was loaded up with food to replenish the stockmen's stores. Beyond the homestead, the plains spread out for ever, and the silence and emptiness were immense. Any sound was sharp and clear as if magnified, and Chris found herself acutely aware of colour, light, texture. All her senses seemed sharpened, but she had also a frightening sense of her own smallness and insignificance and helplessness. Dan was a quiet companion, but she had tremendous confidence in him as she looked about her with a feeling compounded of awe and fear and a kind of excitement. She couldn't help thinking of the early pioneers, and of the women who had come out here with their men. Involuntarily, she thought, 'This land is full of ghosts...'

Dan drove unhesitatingly along what seemed to Chris to be a non-existent track, and soon they were passing through a low forest of blue-grey mulga whose branches had swept the earth beneath quite clear. Bush flowers appeared here and there, the golden yellow of needlewoods, mauve-flowering wild cress, tiny star-faced everlastings and fragile bluebells. Then there were black oaks and beefwood and saltbush, red sands sweeping down to the bed of a dried up creek. And now stunted box trees that grew around a great shallow swamp.

'When the rain comes down here, it's a lake,' Dan told her. 'Right now we're suffering near-drought conditions and the water level's pretty low.'

When Chris looked back, she saw an emu racing along on the far side of the swamp, and a dry buck bush tumbling over and over in slow motion. High above an eagle wheeled against the blue of the sky.

Presently they reached the stock camp. Spare saddles hung from low branches of trees, and on the ground, in the shade, the stockmen's gear lay about—rolled blankets and quart pots and other dusty paraphernalia. Smoke from a dying fire curled lazily upwards and nearby the camp cook was cleaning up. A few hobbled horses were grazing around, and further off a great restless mob of cattle moved in a slow cloud of red dust, watched over by a couple of aboriginal stockmen on well-bred-looking horses. There was no sign of the musterers, who must have been further into the scrub. Chris stayed in the jeep while Dan and the cook unloaded the stores. She thought it a pitiless scene, the heat, the smoke, the dust, the ground worn almost bare from the trampling of the cattle. And those shoddy little piles of personal belongings under the trees. It was a very masculine, very rough and tough sort of camp and she did not belong there. When Dan presently came back from the camp 'kitchen', where he had gone with the cook, and offered her a pannikin of black tea, she asked him tensely, 'Is Burton out here?'

'Burton's on Saltbush Flat. With Paddy,' he said with a look of plain surprise as if she should have known this without being told.

'Paddy?' Chris persisted.

'The overseer.'

'Oh,' said Chris lamely. She felt foolish—and had been made to look so by Burton. He should have clued her up a little, if only for the sake of appearances. The last two nights, he had come back to the homestead late and weary and dust-stained, with hardly a word for her. After dinner, he had gone to the office, and that was all she had seen of him. She wondered now where Saltbush Flat was, and vaguely remembered his saying he would go there to see if Paddy was 'fooling about'. She wondered too if it was a more agreeable place than this, but calculated that most places around Red Sands would be hot, bare, and fairly desolate. She drank her tea thirstily, and although it was very strong, and far too sweet, it was like nectar. She thought irrelevantly, 'One could die of thirst out here very easily.'

Back at the homestead later, she showered, letting the soft lukewarm water run over her hot dusty body. She reflected that it was a strange place to have come to, to pick up the pieces of her life. She had never been anywhere like this before.

She was in a cane lounger on the cool side of the verandah when Burton came in, weary-looking, his face streaked with red dust and sweat. His khaki shirt was crumpled and his hair darkened with perspiration. He stood a few feet off, looking at her.

'What a picture of beauty and indolence! All you lack is

an iced drink, Christine. If you hang on a bit, I'll join you and we'll remedy that.'

She was not altogether sure that she wanted him to do just that, but it was his home. She thought, 'I'll ask him about the girl he hinted was chasing him.' But when it came to the point she didn't.

He appeared in a remarkably short time, the sun-bleached streaks in his brown hair darkened from the shower, his shirt and trousers immaculate. But there were still deep lines of weariness about his eyes, and Chris wondered what had caused them. What did he do out at Saltbush Flat all day? He had brought a tray holding ice, glasses, lemon juice in a jug, a bottle of gin, and one of whisky. He poured gin and squash for Christine, and served himself with whisky, sank into a chair and asked her baldly, 'What did you do with your time today?'

'I went out to the Five Mile Swamp with Dan.'

He gave a quick frown. 'How did that happen? I thought you were relaxing around the homestead.'

'Did you? I'm a healthy girl, whatever you think. Dan thought I might like to see further than the garden.'

'And did you like what you saw?'

'Well,' said Chris consideringly, 'I didn't exactly *like* it. Dust and more dust, emus and tumbleweed. I even saw a mirage! It made me wonder about the people who lived here in the early days—the women in particular. It's—it's a land of ghosts.' She was not sure what made her say that, it was no more than a feeling she had had out there on the plains, but she could see Burton didn't like it. His brows came down darkly, and he turned his glass in his hands, and said nothing for a good ten seconds. When he finally spoke, it was to change the subject completely.

'By the way, we shall have to do something about a ring.'

'A ring? What ring?'

'Our engagement ring, of course.' He looked up and there was a slight smile on his lips. 'Are you pretending to be dense, or have you forgotten our engagement?'

Chris said stiffly, 'We're not engaged. And I'd rather not

37

have a ring.'

'I'd rather you did have a ring. An outward sign speaks louder than words—particularly to the female of the species. As well as that, of course, there's Dan.'

Chris looked at him, not sure if he was laughing or not.

'I don't know what you mean by that. But I know Dan is married. He told me about his wife.'

'He did? Well. I shan't ask what he told you, it's not my department. But I've a ring you can wear, and wear it you shall.'

'For a phoney engagement?'

'That will make it real. Frith will be coming home soon, and Frith is gimlet-eyed.'

'Frith? Your sister?'

'That's right. I don't believe I know any other women called Frith. Do you?'

Chris passed over that. 'I thought she worked in Adelaide.'

'So she does. And I'm only guessing, but Frith does have a habit of coming home when there are other girls around. It's a great shame she hasn't made up her mind to marry that cousin of yours.'

'I didn't know it was so serious.'

He moved restlessly. 'I was hoping it was.' At a slight sound in the house, he turned his head. 'Is that you, Mrs Perry?'

'Yes, Burton. Did you want me?' The housekeeper appeared from a side door that opened into the sitting room. She had a bowl of freshly arranged flowers in her hands, purple lassiandra, trailing stems of jasmine, their yellow flowers shining among the dark leaves.

'Sure I wanted you—I'm slipping, I've just remembered it's mail day.'

'Yes. I'll bring you the letters from the office. I thought you might want to talk to Christine undisturbed.'

He gave her an affectionate smile and she beamed back at him, her plain face acquiring an unexpected radiance. 'I did, old dear. But tell me first—that load of stuff for Saltbush Flat—did that eventuate?'

'The paints and furnishing materials? Yes, Burton. It's all out in the store. Do you want Dan to take it over to-morrow?'

He narrowed his eyes. 'No, I'll do that myself. Now let's have those letters, will you? See what you've done to me, Christine?' he went on as the housekeeper departed. 'You've put me right off my stroke. I'd clean forgotten mail day for once in my life. Mrs Perry will be telling herself that that's Love—with a capital L.'

'Mrs Perry will be wrong, won't she?' said Christine, unamused. 'And anyhow, I think it's ——'

'Unfair to deceive my devoted housekeeper? I shouldn't worry. She's getting no end of a kick out of all this. There've been times when she's despaired of ever seeing me married. But I imagine she's still in the process of deciding whether or not you'll do—and if she decides you won't, then I warn you she can be pretty ruthless.'

'It's happened before, has it?' Christine gave him a cool smile. 'You've been engaged before?' That was a slip—and he was amused at it. All the same——

'Not engaged,' he said, tilting her a smile. He sat back in his chair with a reminiscent look. 'No, not exactly engaged. But on the point of it, let's face it, more than once—in my wild youth.'

'Well, *that*'s long past,' said Chris, unable to resist it.

He laughed out loud. 'It is indeed. I'm thirty-five. And that, let me hasten to point it out to you, is *not* old enough to be your father. Is it, Mrs Perry?' he asked, as the house-keeper reappeared this time with the mail.

'Certainly not!' She told Chris, 'It's not so easy to meet exactly the right girl when you're as isolated as we are on Red Sands. Plenty of men in the outback don't marry till they're going on for forty ... Here's the mail, Burton.' She handed him a tied packet and smiled gently at Christine whose cheeks were red with embarrassment. 'There, isn't that a pretty sight, Burton? I've made her blush. She has that fine clear skin that colours up so easily. You'll have to see she looks after it.'

Burton gave Chris a mocking look that Mrs Perry did not see. 'Beautiful, isn't she, old dear?' he said casually, and began to sort the letters rapidly. One he put in the pocket of his clean white shirt—a letter in a pale pink envelope. The rest he put in neat, small piles. 'I'll deal with those in the office later on. Nothing for you, Christine.' Then, when they were alone, 'I guess the congratulations will begin pouring in pretty soon, though.'

'I haven't told anyone I'm engaged,' said Chris coldly.

'Only your Aunt Patricia,' he said mockingly. 'From the way she greeted me the other day, I can't really think she'll keep it all to herself ... Excuse me, will you?' He produced the pink envelope and slit it open. Chris caught the whiff of some flowery scent as he unfolded the pages. Through her lashes she watched as he read it, and saw an odd smile curl the edges of his mouth.

Who was it from? she wondered. Was it from the girl on his tail? But she had had the impression that that girl was out here at Red Sands. He glanced up as he refolded the letter and put it back in his pocket, and caught her out in her veiled stare. She asked, disconcerted, 'Is it from Frith?'

'Frith won't write. She believes in shock tactics,' he said unrevealingly. He heaved himself out of his chair and stood, tall and brown and broad-shouldered, looking down at her enigmatically. He was not going to tell her who that letter was from, and she felt rebuffed. Even rebuked. She could not expect the rights of a genuine fiancée. 'I'll see you about that ring later, Christine.'

'No, you won't,' thought Chris as she watched him stride off along the verandah. She had very mixed feelings about the whole concern. She could not deny that there was a magnetic quality about Burton Alexander's personality. Several times, she had found herself watching him, listening to him, pondering over how different he was out here at Red Sands from the man whom she had met in Adelaide. That man had been strikingly good-looking, well-groomed, and self-assured. A man who enjoyed classical music and was perfectly home in a smart restaurant, a night club, or in the fashionable parts of the city. Out here, his good looks acquired a rugged, ruthless quality. One was conscious of the muscular strength of his broad shoulders, his tanned arms; of the authority concealed behind casually issued orders, of the responsibility that made those lines of weariness and strain around his eyes. She wondered what was going on at Saltbush Flat. Paddy was supposed to be moving stock from there, Burton was taking a hand in it himself. Then stores in the form of paints and furnishing materials had arrived for Saltbush Flat. Burton had said he would take them over, rather than Dan, and Chris had had the feeling that it had occurred to him that if Dan went, he might take her with him. But why should he want to keep her away from Saltbush Flat? Why?

While they drank their coffee that night after dinner, Burton strolled over to the piano and began to play a Schubert Impromptu. He smiled over his shoulder at Chris once or twice as he played, and Mrs Perry gave the two of them a fond indulgent look. Chris felt an uncomfortable urge to dissociate herself from the soft romantic music, the low lamplight. They had nothing to do with her. She refused to look at Burton, and even tried not to listen, however beguiling the music. She allowed herself to be distracted by Dan who, having set down his coffee cup, had begun to roll a cigarette. He looked as if he was hardly aware of his surroundings, there was a frown on his forehead, and Chris was sure he was thinking of his wife and worrying about her.

From a small side table, the photograph of a woman looked out enigmatically and remotely. Chris had looked at that photograph before. It was of a pretty young woman—scarcely more than a girl—with large, slightly tilted eyes, soft fair hair and a wistful expression on her high-cheekboned face. It had taken some time to realise that it reminded her of Frith Alexander. She had met Frith only two or three times, and somehow could not associate her with the world of Red Sands.

Presently, while Burton still played absorbedly, there was another distraction. The little boy Jason came to the door in his pyjamas, a tearful look on his face. He ran to Mrs Perry, buried his face in her lap and began to sob, 'I want my mummy!'

Dan was there at once, to pick him up and tell him firmly, 'Don't cry, son. Mummy will soon be back. Come and I'll tell you a story.' As he left the room, Chris followed quietly in his wake. She felt a helpless pity for the man and the child, but she knew there was nothing she, a stranger, could do. Her escape was a selfish one, on her own behalf. Her nerves were too taut to stand much more of that music, aware as she was of Burton's glances and of Mrs Perry's approval. Besides, she was afraid Burton would bring up the subject of the ring again, and she was determined to avoid him.

Outside the sitting room, she asked Dan sympathetically, 'Is there anything I can do?'

'Afraid not, Christine. Only Peg will do.'

They parted and she went down the hallway round the corner, and opened the door into her bedroom. At almost exactly the same instant, Burton appeared at the door that led on to the verandah, and they stood confronting each other across the room in the half dark.

Burton said, his tone peremptory, 'Come out here, Christine.'

Chris bit her lip. 'I'm tired. I'm going to bed.'

'I shan't keep you all that long.'

'What do you want?'

'It's that little matter of our engagement ring.'

'I don't want it,' said Chris flatly.

'That's too bad. I want you to start wearing it now. Will you come out here and receive it decently and conventionally, or must I hold you down on that soft cushy-looking bed and force it on to your finger?'

Chris said angrily, 'It's a stupid situation. Why can't we forget it?'

'You chose it yourself,' said Burton, one eyebrow cocked

wearily. His blue eyes looked at her levelly and disconcertingly across the room, for in a sort of panic she had switched on the ceiling light. 'And I need a fiancée right now.'

'I don't think you do at all.'

'No?' The other eyebrow went up. 'Then what do you suppose this is all about?'

Chris felt baffled. 'There's no other girl out here.'

'Sweetheart, believe me there is. You'll meet her when the time's good and ripe, and you're more at home in your role.' He held out his hand. 'Come along now. Switch off that light and step on to the verandah and we'll do the thing with decorum. Otherwise'—his eyes suddenly darkened menacingly—'by heaven, I'll pick you up and——'

Chris didn't wait for him to finish. She flicked off the light and bounded past him through the door, to stand panting at the verandah rail. The scent of the yellow jasmine was sickly sweet in her nostrils, shadows from the palm trees fell across the pale fabric of her dress, making slashes like stains on its purity. A half moon floated high in a purple sky that was dazed and dewy with stars, and the Milky Way drifted like a silver mist.

'The aboriginals call it the smoke from God's campfire,' said Burton softly, following her gaze. His voice was too close, too intimate, she felt a faint shiver pass over her limbs. Agonised, she longed for the familiarity of Francis at her side, for Francis's voice with its French intonations saying—oh, thought Chris wildly, afraid of tears, saying anything at all to her—calling her Chérie as he had called her a thousand thousand times. Chérie—*ma chérie*——

Burton reached for her left hand. 'We'll see if it fits.'

'Please —' She snatched her hand away.

'For God's sake! Is it tender memories again? Don't tell me the finger that wore Francis Rogeon's ring is sacred.' His fingers, strong and inescapable, were around her two wrists, and he began easing her round to face him. He held her still and stared hard and cynically down into her face, his own blue-shadowed in the moonlight and slashed weirdly by the shadows of palm leaves that scurried in a faint frenzy as a fugitive and furtive night wind lifted them.

Chris's voice was husky, ragged. 'I've never worn a ring——'

'What?' He stopped in mid-movement his slow and liquid spinning of her. 'No ring? A broken heart, but—no broken engagement?'

'That's right,' breathed Chris, fighting tears.

'Then all your fuss is over a dream. I thought this man of yours had jilted you—that it was all real.'

Chris bit hard on her lip, blinked quickly to clear away her tears. Words were ready to tumble from her mouth—accusations of lack of understanding on his part, assertions of true love on her own. But where would it get her? She heard herself say clearly, venomously, 'I would like to bite you—to scratch your eyes out——'

'Christine, Christine!' She could see the whiteness of his teeth as he smiled, actually smiled. She could see the glint of amusement in his eyes. But he said reasonably—hatefully reasonably—'You mustn't take it so hard—you must certainly do something about yourself. You must forget what's over and beyond mending.'

How easy it sounded! And how little he knew about love! Chris had tried and tried to come to terms with herself, to accept what had happened. She had lain awake night after night reasoning with herself, repeating to herself the futility of wishing it had all happened differently. But it always came back to a very elementary fact: Her heart was sore and aching. And that, apparently, was something Burton Alexander could simply not understand.

She had closed her eyes as if to hide herself, and now she could feel his warm breath, feel his dark shadow coming between herself and the moon. His lips touched hers lightly and then with increasing pressure, his hands released her wrists one at a time as he pulled her bodily against him ...

'Did he kiss you like that, Christine? There's a saying that a new kiss will wipe out the old——'

Chris pulled away and put the back of her hand to her mouth, and he said wryly, philosophically, 'Well, there's a beginning—a single drop of water. I'm sorry about that. And still sorrier that you must wear my ring just now. Put it on and forget all about it. Here, do the deed yourself if you prefer it that way. But do it now—I shan't give you till tomorrow.'

He spoke lightly enough, but Chris knew that he meant what he said. He had a habit of speaking with an air of authority that was unmistakable, and she simply didn't know how to contest it.

'Come along now,' he said almost sharply as she stood motionless, silent. 'It's a business matter quite simply. Payment for being allowed to stay here. I'll leave you alone, I assure you.'

'Thank you,' she managed, her lips stiff. She had begun to shiver. She took the ring and slipped it on to her finger, and of course it meant nothing and didn't matter in the least. She even wondered why she had made such a to-do, been so melodramatic.

'That's a good girl,' said Burton approvingly. 'Goodnight. Sleep well.'

He was gone, and she was left alone. She stood for two or three minutes, her mind blank, waiting for her shivering fit to subside, and then she went into her bedroom and switched on the reading lamp. She looked at the ring on her finger. The stone in it was a very beautiful ruby and it burned like red fire. 'It's beautiful,' she thought, distracted. She held out her hand and looked at her long, square-tipped fingers. For the fraction of a second her mind held the thought—'If only Francis had given me this'—and then she told herself flatly, 'It's a business matter,' and remembered that Burton had promised to leave her alone.

But had he meant tonight—or always?

She slept badly that night, and got up before the sun had risen, hearing voices and movements. There was a slight chill in the air, but she got out of bed and scrambled into jeans and a shirt, thinking that she would discover what

45

went on at Red Sands in the early morning. She tied back her red hair quickly, and caught sight of the ruby flashing on her left hand. She murmured a fierce, almost silent, 'No!'—negating it, asking Francis, or the ghost of Francis, to forgive her...

As she hurried towards the kitchen, she heard Mrs Perry talking to Burton. 'Don't forget those paints and stuff for Saltbush Flat, Burton. And there's lettuce in the basket, and fresh carrots and tomatoes, and some eggs. And I've cooked a nice little brisket of beef.'

'Good heavens!' came Burton's amused comment. 'You must think the girl has a phenomenal appetite! Either that, or that she's got nothing to do but eat. But thanks, old dear, you're a living wonder.'

Chris stood quite still in the hallway. Outside in the yard she could hear someone moving—possibly Joe, who looked after the machinery and the lighting system and was always around the homestead. Then she heard Burton walk along the verandah, the slam of the screen door. A moment later, a motor started up, and Burton was off to Saltbush Flat. And to the girl who lived there.

The girl on his tail?

CHAPTER THREE

SHE knew she would not rest until she had met that girl. Burton had said, 'You'll meet her when you're more at home in your role,' but now Chris felt restless. She wanted to meet that girl *now*. All day, she found it impossible to settle to anything. Mrs Perry was making bread and she went to the kitchen to watch her.

'We get bread every week from town,' the housekeeper told her, busy with the dough. 'But Burton likes my bread and so do the stockmen. It's a change for them from the camp cook's damper when they're away mustering. Dan always takes a batch out when he goes with the supplies.'

'Where's Jason today?' Chris wanted to know. The little boy was generally somewhere round about the kitchen in the mornings.

'He's gone out with Dan to Copper Burr Bore. Harry's been having some trouble with the pump out there and Burton asked Dan to check it over. He can do a bit of everything, Dan can. It meant an early start today.' She gave Chris a look that was a little apologetic, as though she too thought what Chris was thinking—that Burton was making sure Chris did not go anywhere with Dan today.

Chris asked absently, 'Does Dan take the supplies over to Saltbush Flat too?'

'Oh, Burton sees to Saltbush.' Mrs Perry sighed as she packed the last of the sweet-smelling yeasty dough into the long tins, and covered it with a cloth. 'It's a real shame that sale fell through after all the trouble and time Burton spent on it. All those weeks in Adelaide, too. Still and all, it's an ill wind—it meant he could see more of you, didn't it?'

'Yes,' said Chris, half ashamed of her deceit. She remembered that Burton had been arranging to buy some property or other when first she met him. She had assumed he had put the deal through, and it was something of a surprise now to learn that it was Saltbush Flat he had been negotiating to buy. She had thought it was part of the estate, just as Five Mile Swamp and Copper Burr Bore were, but it appeared that he had not been able to buy it after all. He had never discussed any of his business affairs with her, and of course they did not concern her. 'All the same,' thought Chris, moving moodily about the kitchen and looking at the various enormous pans and stirring spoons that Mrs Perry had hanging on the wall, 'he'll have to clue me up a bit if I'm to meet this girl and act as if I was engaged to marry him.' She thought it a pity that Burton did not put in some time tutoring her instead of giving her rings or preaching to her on the undesirability of suffering from a broken heart.

'I suppose you're finding it a bit lonely and quiet here,' Mrs Perry said into the little silence that had fallen between them. 'Most of the stockmen are at the muster at Five Mile Swamp, and then there's this business of shifting the fats off Saltbush. Paddy Preston's in charge of that.'

'He's Burton's overseer, isn't he?' ventured Chris, frowning a little as she made an effort to put herself in the picture.

'That's right. But I don't expect you'll see much of Paddy. He spends most of his time at the muster camps and that's the way he likes it. He's a real outback man, is Paddy.' She opened the door of the big oven to look at some cakes she was baking, and added inconsequentially, 'A handsome fellow. A favourite with Frith, I always think, though he never has much time for her, and just as well.'

'Why do you say that, Mrs Perry?'

The housekeeper, her face flushed from the heat of the oven, became non-committal. 'Well, Frith's not really a country girl. Besides, Burton wouldn't like it.'

Chris wondered why not, but somehow she couldn't ask Mrs Perry about *that*. It would seem odd, when a girl in her position could ask Burton himself. Instead, she asked idly, 'How far is it to Saltbush Flat, Mrs Berry?'

'Oh, no more than fifteen or eighteen miles, dear—to the old homestead, that is. It's a good way further to where the men are mustering. Saltbush Flat is one of nature's freaks. I don't know what Burton's going to do without it, I'm sure. It's a real shame the lease has expired and he has to shift those cattle back on to Red Sands. They'll lose so much condition it'll be nobody's business.'

Chris felt baffled by her own ignorance, and annoyed with Burton for allowing her to be ignorant. She wandered off presently, fetched her hat, and went purposefully to the saddling yard. There she leaned over the rails and took a good look at the few horses there. She picked out a little grey that she liked the look of and later on—after lunch and after she had taken a siesta, for it was sizzlingly hot—she

48

asked Joe to saddle the grey for her. She had always enjoyed riding and decided to try out the little mare first as far as the waterhole, and then, if they got on well together, to go on from there. Right now, she didn't know the direction to take for Saltbush Flat, and at all events it was too late to go today. But she would go tomorrow, early in the morning. The idea livened her up considerably, and it occupied most of her attention as she let the mare, Sally, canter over the sandy flats and along the creek bank.

She did not once think of Francis until as she pulled on the reins she caught the glint of the ruby on her finger. It seemed crazy that that ring should remind her of Francis, but it did, and she wondered what he was doing now, and if he ever thought of her, and before she knew it she was back on the old treadmill. If only things had been different—if only Pam had never come to work at Millunga—if only her own mother hadn't been ill and she hadn't had to go away from the vineyard ...

Sally ambled along the dry creek bed, and with an abrupt effort, Chris brought her thoughts to a halt. She was sick and tired of thinking the same old things, over and over and over. In a minute, she would be right in the middle of another fit of depression and self-pity, and she was tired of that too. It was the first time she had looked at herself and her reactions so dispassionately, and she felt more than a little surprised. Maybe, she thought unemotionally, it was the way Burton had said. Francis had simply decided to make sensible marriage. And if he could do that—poor Pam!

Sally began to canter friskily, and ahead Chris could see the shining strip that was the waterhole, green and clear under the high blue sky. Around it, trees leaned down to their reflections and a couple of little blue bonnets flirted about. The sunlight was still dazzling, and the air was very still. A heat haze shimmered over the plain, a few boulders caught the light glintingly, an eagle soared high high up in a sky so blue it seemed to have no ending. Beyond the waterhole, faint wheel tracks went across the plain, possibly made by the mail van as it went on to the next cattle station, Flora Creek. Chris felt suddenly curious about the Flora Creek people, but she hoped too that she would not have to meet them. It would only mean more people to deceive. She wondered how many people knew about Burton's engagement. Perhaps by the time the muster was over and the stockmen back at the homestead the whole charade would have ended and she would be free. But she had a feeling that Burton would insist she stay until she had performed whatever service he required of her.

'Crazy!' muttered Chris to herself, allowing Sally to canter over those wheel tracks in the red earth that was baked hard by the sun. It seemed like rehearsing for a play that was never to be put on! She felt quite determined that tomorrow she would go to Saltbush Flat and meet the girl there—the girl to whom Burton was taking fresh garden vegetables and a 'nice little brisket of beef'. Now she knew that Sally was amiable and easy to handle, she would watch to see which way Burton came home this evening and tomorrow morning she would be off before the sun was too hot ...

She wandered around the verandah restlessly when she went back to the homestead, then went into the garden and through to the gravel yard where the cars came in. It seemed ages before at last she saw a small cloud of dust spiralling up into the sky out on the flat horizon to the south-east. Eventually, it turned out to be Burton's jeep. So, thought Chris, that was the way to Saltbush Flat! There would be tracks to follow, and she would make it all right ...

Burton was tired and dusty and not in the best of tempers when he climbed out of the jeep and saw her standing in the yard smiling at him. He came towards her slowly, his eyes glittering and screwed up, and she could see perspiration streaks marking the red dust that lay on his cheeks and forehead.

'For the lord's sake, Christine, don't start meeting me the minute I come in! Give me time to shower and change. I'm not fit to be welcomed in my present condition and not fit to lay hands on you.'

Chris looked at him with clear eyes as he stood, his hands on his narrow hips, his feet slightly apart, squinting down at her with a savage intensity. His utter masculinity was peculiarly fascinating. He was completely unlike Francis, and there was a magnetism about him that held her gaze so that it required a definite effort for her to turn her head slightly, to blink, to tell him caustically as though suddenly awakened, 'I'm not here to welcome you. I just happened to come out into the yard at the wrong time.'

His own gaze did not shift. It remained narrow and concentrated. He said briefly, 'Is that so?' And then abruptly, as if dismissing her completely, he strode off towards the homestead.

She did not see him again until dinner time. Usually in the evenings after he had showered and changed he went into the sitting room for a drink or to play the piano. Mrs Perry said it renewed him, and she meant both the music and the drink, but tonight he went to the office and was there with Dan until the housekeeper knocked on the door and said dinner was ready.

After dinner, he sat out on the verandah. Mrs Perry went to her own small sitting room to listen to the radio, Dan had gone to his quarters or to look in on Jason, and Chris was left alone with Burton. She sat, oddly self-conscious, in a chair three feet away from his and looked out across the garden and the night as he was doing. She gave a little start when he asked her abruptly, 'Do you find time to be lonely, Christine? Or is your mind too fully occupied with dwelling on the past?' He didn't wait for her to answer, but continued bracingly, 'You must get ready to snap out of it—my sister will be here any day now.'

'Why? Because of Paddy?' Chris was not sure why she said that, except to keep the limelight off herself, but she saw a hard look come over his face.

'Who's been telling you about Paddy and Frith? Because, I assure you, there's nothing to tell.'

'Isn't there?' Chris remembered Mrs Perry's casual remarks. 'I thought he might be the reason why she isn't going to marry my cousin Richard.'

'Then you're mistaken,' he said coldly.

'Is there something wrong with Paddy?' Chris insisted innocently. She knew that he was annoyed and it gave her a kind of pleasure to needle him. 'I should like to meet him.'

'No doubt you'll do just that one of these days. You might even find him fascinating by that time. Most girls up from the city do. But he's a man in a man's world, and women are no more than an amusement to him.'

He looked at her hard, and Chris said with a glint in her grey eyes, 'You're warning me to remember that when the time comes.'

His eyebrows went up cynically and the dent at the corner of his mouth showed briefly. 'I'm not quite sure that I need to warn you, Christine. You're a special case. It all depends on the state of your health when the momentous meeting takes place ... Now tell me what you did with yourself today.'

Chris, who didn't particularly like his reference to the state of her health, answered quickly, 'I got Joe to saddle up Sally for me and I took a look at the waterhole and round and about.' She was gratified to see she had surprised him, but his comment was slightly sarcastic.

'Wonderful! Though you could have walked to the swimming hole quite easily. Did you go in for a dip?'

'No. I went out for the ride.'

'You like horses, do you?'

'Yes.' Chris wondered if he would file that little bit of information and use it later in company, to make his role of lover more convincing.

'Fine. You must do all the riding you like. It'll be a healthier way of amusing yourself than moping about the house all day.'

'If you knew the least thing about me,' said Chris hotly, stung by the unjustness of his implication, 'you'd know that's one thing I'd never do——'

'Never?' He eyed her quizzically and disconcertingly. 'I thought that was how you put in most of your time in Adelaide. But we'll forget it, if you want it that way ... What used you to do all day in that valley of yours in New South Wales?'

'I don't see why I should tell you,' said Chris. 'Besides, you keep telling me I should forget it—that it's all past.'

'So it is. And for you, that could be one way of putting it all well and truly in the past, sweetheart. You talk about it enough to me and I'll guarantee that pretty soon it'll seem as dead as the dodo to you. Like a piece of verse you've recited once or twice too often ... So what used you to do?'

Chris studied him for a moment. His attitude annoyed her more than she could say and she really had no idea how to retaliate. To sulk—to be silent—to shed tears—none of those would defeat him. And she simply couldn't be bothered getting up and walking away. Finally, as he looked back at her as steadily as she was looking at him, completely expressionless except for a faint tilting of his brows—she said lightly, 'Nothing that would seem very exciting to—to someone like you. I used to spend a lot of time at Francis's vineyard, maybe do a bit of gardening for him, or go down among the vines with him.' She stopped abruptly, aware that a note of softness, of weakness, of nostalgia had crept into her voice as she remembered those days that now seemed like no more than a dream, they were gone so completely.

'Hmm,' said Burton after a second. 'And down among the vines, he would declaim on the poetry of the grape and the romance of wine-making, I assume. Or was he a practical man through and through?' He leaned across and took her left hand, raising it into the shaft of light that fell through the doorway behind them. 'There are wines that are as red as the ruby and as luscious and as lovely. But pretty soon if we're careful with you, when you look at that ring, Christine, you'll see a ruby instead of a drop of wine.' He dropped her hand. 'But we shan't rush our fences.

You're still pretty sick.'

'Well, if *you* say so,' said Chris tartly. She thought of her decision to go to Saltbush Flat tomorrow, but she was not going to tell him about that. He might easily decide to put a stop to it. She yawned ostentatiously and rose. 'If you'll excuse me, Burton, I'll go to bed—much as I've been enjoying our conversation.'

He gave her a sharp look. 'Run along, then. I shan't kiss you goodnight. But watch out for your dreams.'

She had no idea what he meant by that. At all events, she had no dreams that night—or none that she could remember.

She was up a little earlier than usual in the morning, and told Mrs Perry casually after breakfast, 'I'm going for a ride—out Saltbush way. Could I have some sandwiches and fruit to take with me?'

'Yes, of course. You should have got up earlier and gone with Burton. Though just now he's too busy shifting the cattle off that lease to have time for much else. It's a great shame.'

It was hot as Chris set off from the homestead. She had a waterbottle and some food in her saddle bag, and she wore a stockman's hat that she had got from the stores. Dan was doing the books that morning, and Chris didn't tell him where she was going when she asked for the hat. She had told Mrs Perry and that was enough. She knew it was wrong to set off on a journey of any kind in this outback country without telling someone where you were making for. Not that she imagined anything would happen to her, but just suppose she did have an accident of some kind, she would be on the track that led to Saltbush Flat and Burton would find her.

It wasn't long before the perspiration was running down the back of her neck, and she pushed her long red hair up inside her hat. 'If I lived out here,' she reflected, 'I'd wear it short.' She let Sally canter for a while to get the freshness out of her, but it was not long before the mare slowed to a walk. The track was easy enough to follow through the low forest of mulga that covered the plain and filtered over the long low red hills. Chris had time to look about her and she saw little bush flowers like flickering lights as their colour flared through the indigo shadows on the red ground—bluebells, yellow boronia, the bright flame of the wild fuchsia. The sun rose higher and higher in the blueness of the sky and all around was a kind of ticking silence. She saw no cattle, and not a thing moved except for the shimmering waters of a wide lake that never got any closer. A mirage. The track she followed skirted around boulders, wove through thick clumps of saltbush, curved around a low spur, and then continued across the desolate flat of a saltpan. After a long, long time, there was a five-wire cattle fence, and the track finally led to a gate. Chris dismounted to open it and was careful to close it behind her. She thought with a feeling of excitement that she must now be on Saltbush Flat. The track followed the wire fence, and Chris rode steadily on while the sun beat down on her fiercely, its heat growing more and more enervating as the morning wore on.

It was wild, empty, hungry-looking country, and she couldn't see why Mrs Perry had referred to it as a 'freak of nature'. It seemed to Chris to be exactly the same as what she had seen of Red Sands, only somehow emptier, half deserted. For the life of her, she couldn't see why Burton Alexander had ever wanted to lease this land or why he had put any of his cattle here.

Ahead of her, the track branched into two. One fork continued on along the fence, the other curved off and rounded a spur. Chris chose the second one, and to her relief and pleasure, as she came around the spur she saw Saltbush Flat homestead and its few surrounding outhouses, some distance away. But even from afar, she could see quite plainly that the outhouses were definitely coming apart at the seams. They didn't look as though they had been used for years and years. The weather had dried them up, and the winds were blowing them slowly but surely apart.

The homestead was a different matter. Pink-flowering

oleanders and untidy clumps of bamboo grew close about it and gave it shade and shelter, and soon Chris caught sight of someone in the garden, stooping in the narrow strip of noonday shade that edged the verandah. It was a girl in a flimsy-looking pink straw hat with a wide floppy brim, and as Chris rode closer she straightened, lifting a huge watering can from the ground. At the sound of the horse's hooves, she turned and stared across the garden at Chris.

For some reason Chris's heart had begun to race, and suddenly she wondered what she did next. She hadn't really thought ahead as far as this point—as far as actually meeting the girl out here. Her ruby ring flashed fire in the sun as she pulled on the reins to bring Sally to a standstill. She slid to the ground and walked towards the girl feeling doubtful, and very much aware that she was not engaged to Burton Alexander at all.

The girl in the pink hat set her watering can down again, called out a very welcoming, 'Hi!' and came to the white gate that had fallen away from its hinges at the top and was lurching tipsily against a dusty, prickly-looking hedge.

Chris called back, 'Hello!' and wondered whether she should tether Sally to a tree or whether that would look as if she had come to call. But of course, in the outback one always did come to call, and the girl at the gate said, 'Leave your horse. I'll tell Billy to take care of it. Come on in and let's get acquainted.' There was only a couple of yards between them now, and Chris saw that she was a very small girl, not much over five feet tall. She was looking at Chris curiously from round very blue eyes surrounded by long obviously false eyelashes. Blonde curls had escaped from under her hat whose wide brim shed a soft rosy light—very flattering—on cheeks that were already pink. Chris thought she looked about sixteen, and very ingenuous.

'Now let me guess who you are,' said this pretty childlike creature. '*Red* hair. You just can't be *Frith*?'

'No, I'm——'

'Don't tell me! Let me guess, it's more fun.' The blue eyes made a quick journey to Chris's left hand and back, and the pretty soft mouth formed an 'O!' Then—'You're *Christine!*'

'Yes. Christine Vance. I'm sorry, but I don't know your name——'

The girl looked comically hurt, 'I'm Jackie—Jackie Lester. Come inside out of the sun—you look so *hot*—and we'll have a cup of tea and get acquainted. Your horse will be all right. Honestly—I'll tell Billy right away. You go ahead—go right inside where it's *cool*, and make yourself at home.'

Chris obeyed with a feeling of apprehension. Jackie Lester. And she knew Chris's name—or part of it at least. But could this *child* be the girl from whom Burton needed protection? This small, blue-eyed, ingenuous-looking blonde child? Surely a man with Burton Alexander's experience would simply eat her up! She would present no problem——

Chris stepped across the verandah and went through the open door into the dimness of the house. There were signs of chaos—furniture had been moved into the wide hallway, and the room at the front that should have been the sitting room was empty except for a wooden kitchen chair, a stepladder, a pail of water, and a cloth. Even the floor was bare. Chris stood helplessly in the doorway and waited for the little blonde who presently joined her and linked one arm companionably—and irritatingly, somehow—through hers. Chris would have liked to disengage herself, but for the moment forbore.

'I've made a start on that room,' said Jackie Lester with a small grimace. 'Ugh! Those old walls are so hideous! Uncle Arthur was a dear, but he didn't have any taste, did he? I couldn't live with that ugly old creamy yellow colour —it reminds me too much of school. We'll go out to the side verandah—Lena's made a salad and there's some cold beef. There's plenty for two.'

Chris put aside thoughts of the picnic lunch Mrs Perry had packed for her and followed the other girl down a dim hallway, past closed doors, and on to a narrow verandah where a small table covered with a green and white checked cloth stood against the wall. Soon they were eating from plain white plates that looked—and were—completely new.

'Everything on Saltbush was so old and cracked—I had plates and things sent out from town,' said Jackie, her guileless blue eyes smiling at Chris.

It was not until the business of eating was over and they were sitting over a second helping of iced orange drink that she admitted, 'I only *heard* about you two days ago. I didn't even know Burton was engaged till then.' She reached out and touched the ruby ring on Chris's finger. 'That's beautiful. And so unusual with red hair.'

Chris looked at her quickly. Was there just a touch of cattiness in that remark? A suggestion that rubies didn't suit red-haired people? Well, it didn't matter to Chris anyway. What Burton had told her came back into her mind: You'll meet the other girl when the time is ripe, and you're more at home in your role. *That* would be never, thought Chris, but determined all the same to make an effort to appear so, if that was what Burton wanted. 'Think of it as a job,' she told herself. Even though Burton had said it wasn't a job. She knew that right now, she ought to say something about that ruby—maybe tell Jackie Lester that they had chosen the ring for sentimental reasons, or because it was her birth stone, or something like that. But it was the sort of glib and easy and meaningless lie that Christine simply could not tell, and so she said nothing. Burton was certainly right in keeping her away from Jackie Lester! She could not convince anyone of the reality of her engagement if she tried—she had simply been lucky that Mrs Perry and Dan Spencer took Burton's word for it that they were going to be married. Though even those two seemed to regard it as being in the experimental stage. Burton and Chris would be married if Chris liked it at Red Sands—if she felt she could settle in the outback ... *This* girl was not going to look on it that way—and Burton didn't want her to.

Jackie was watching her curiously. She reached for cigarettes, looked a question at Chris who shook her head, and lit up.

'What did Burton tell you about *me*?' she asked Chris, as she tilted her head back and blew smoke in a sophisticated way that went oddly with her appearance.

'Nothing,' said Chris simply.

Jackie stared, then gave a little strangled laugh. 'Oh, Christine, I can't believe that! You're just being discreet. Otherwise, why did you come to see me?'

Chris said, knowing that she had reddened, 'I followed some tracks—and landed here.'

'I'll bet you knew they were Burton's tracks and that they'd bring you here. I guess you must have smelt a rat and wanted to find out who he was visiting every day!'

Chris shrugged slightly and shook her head. She was beginning to wonder why she *had* come here—and even to wish a little that she had not. It was pique, perhaps, that Burton hadn't told her more about the girl who was the reason why he needed a fiancée. But was he visiting Jackie every day, as she claimed? If he were, then it seemed odd behaviour from a man who insinuated he needed some sort of protection.

She looked at Jackie and asked mildly, 'Every day? But I didn't know Burton came here every day—except of course to see about his cattle.'

'His cattle—and me. Every day,' said Jackie with a little sigh. Her long, long eyelashes were lowered and lay softly on her pretty pink cheeks. Without her hat, she looked like a doll. Her hair was in such cute blonde curls, and she wore a pink ribbon in it that matched her simple pink cotton dress. She looked up at Chris suddenly and her eyes were not in the least doll-like. 'He's a *gorgeous* hunk of a man, isn't he? I met him in Adelaide last month at old Uncle Arthur's funeral, and I fell flat on my face in love with him in less than a minute. Fancy falling in love at a funeral! But it was a gorgeous funeral—so sort of sadly gay. I loved every single person there, but Burton most of all. Except for him and me and Mummy, everyone was about eighty— all Uncle Arthur's funny old friends. There was even a fantastic old actress gone to seed that Mummy remembered seeing in "Rose Marie" when she was a little girl! And she was crying for Uncle Arthur, black mascara all down her wrinkly old cheeks, and telling marvellous stories about him. She was really sweet. *You* weren't at the funeral, were you, Christine? When did *you* meet Burton?'

Chris felt herself blush deeply. If only she could claim to have known Burton for years, how convincing it would sound! Instead, she admitted, deliberately vague, 'Not so terribly long ago. Frith was friendly with one of my cousins in Adelaide, you see, so——'

'I'm glad it wasn't long ago,' said Jackie with rueful satisfaction. 'I mean, if it was a thing that had been going on for years, I'd feel awful, I really would.' She bit on her full pink underlip and stubbed out her barely smoked cigarette with a kind of childish thoroughness, waiting until the smoke had stopped rising before she looked up again. 'I *would* like to marry Burton, Christine. I'd rather set my heart on it. It's not a very nice thing to tell you, but—well, I mean, the way Burton's behaved, he can't expect anything else, can he? He didn't tell me about you, and he didn't tell you about me, and he hasn't known either of us all that long, has he? I know you have a ring, but still, I think we start about even. He would like to own Saltbush Flat, and it belongs to me.'

Chris blinked and frowned. She was certainly learning things! She knew Burton had wanted to buy Saltbush Flat, but she hadn't known it belonged to Jackie Lester. She was rapidly revising her initial impression of Miss Lester as a little-girl-in-a-garden! She said confusedly, 'Burton can *buy* Saltbush Flat if he really wants it.'

Jackie put her head on one side and appeared to be considering that. Then she said regretfully, 'Maybe he thinks he won't *need* to buy it, Christine. I don't want to hurt your feelings, but I don't think Burton has really made up his mind which of us two he wants the most.' She smiled almost sadly as if she were very sorry to tell Christine this, and Chris thought to herself, 'I could tell you the answer to that one very easily—he doesn't want either of us, and I've been brought to Red Sands specifically to convince you that he doesn't want *you*.'

'You see,' Jackie continued, starting on another cigarette, 'Burton *was* going to buy Saltbush Flat, but he decided not to. He wanted me to come out here so he could get to know me better, I guess—he does come to see me every day, after all. And I expect you're here too so he can make up his mind between us. You have the ring because you've probably got parents or people who wouldn't let you come here unless it was all very proper—you do look that kind of girl, if you don't mind me saying so. When I met Burton at that funeral, he took me and Mummy to lunch afterwards and he said he wanted to buy Saltbush Flat. Uncle Arthur left it to me in his will. I suppose you know all about *that*.' Chris did not know all about it by any means, but she suspected that very soon she would. Jackie was plainly a girl who liked to talk—preferably about herself—so Chris said nothing, but allowed the spate of words to roll on.

'Arthur Lester and my father were sort of cousins, and he took a fancy to me when I was very tiny—before Daddy died, and that's why he left this place to me. I didn't have a clue what to do with it, and William Harrington told me I must sell it.' She stopped and looked speculatively at Chris to make sure she was following.

'Was he your lawyer?' Chris suggested, sitting back in preparation for a long talking session.

'No! He's the man that Mummy's just married. They weren't married then, and he doesn't like me very much, and I just know now that his idea was to sort of get rid of me. I'd be able to support myself you see, if I had all the money this property is worth. There's a whole lot of ore or oil or something on it as well as everything else, I know because some of those old people at the funeral kept talking about it.'

She paused to draw breath, and Chris, who had been listening closely and with quite some interest, tried to sort out her feeling of confusion.

'So of course,' continued Jackie after a few seconds, 'I thought it was the right thing to do. I mean, after all, who'd want to own a place called Saltbush Flat? Imagine the address on your best notepaper—Miss Jacqueline Lester invites you to a party at her home, Saltbush Flat. Well, everyone would laugh themselves sick! Anyhow, Burton and I met and we had talks and Mr Harrington got the lawyer to fix up all the papers and everything because he wanted to get it fixed really quickly so he could marry dear old Mummy and take her to Japan with him and combine a honeymoon with a business trip. As though he had to when he's got just loads of money! I'd have liked to go to Japan too, but he wouldn't hear of taking me. Mummy did suggest it, she's sweet, but the horrid old beast just wouldn't be in it. Not kind! And after all, I mean—people as old as that, more than *forty*, can hardly expect much of a honeymoon!' She stopped and widened her blue eyes. 'Oh, I do hope I'm not boring you?'

'No,' said Chris. 'Please go on.'

'Well, meanest trick of all, Mr Harrington had made Mummy arrange for me to stay with an absolutely dreary old bourgeois aunt—Daddy's oldest sister—and there couldn't be a bigger generation gap in the whole world than there is between me and Aunt Gertrude—no, I mean it! So then'—she looked across the garden and a smile touched her slightly pouting lips—'Burton stepped in and said he'd changed his mind about buying Saltbush Flat and why didn't I come out here and see how I liked the bush instead of staying with Aunt Gertrude. So that's what I did.' Her gaze returned to Chris, guileless and full of innocence. 'He just didn't want me to disappear out of his life before he decided whether or not he wanted to marry me.'

'I see,' said Chris inadequately, and without the least idea how true it all was.

'It's really rather awful when you come to think of it, isn't it?'

Chris wondered whether she would agree, if she were really expecting to marry Burton. She tried for casualness, and asked lightly, 'What's awful about it?'

'Well!' Jackie widened her already enormous eyes. 'I mean—doing things that way. Getting engaged to one girl and inviting another out to see how she likes the bush.' She giggled a little. 'But I guess that's the way Burton is—sort of he-mannish and brutal, and treading on your feelings, and I *love* it.' She looked at Chris doubtfully. 'I don't think *you* do, though. I think you're one of those nicely brought up girls who pretend everything's all right even when they know it isn't. Do you mind me saying that?' She leaned her elbows on the table and looked pensively at Chris through the smoke that drifted from her parted lips. She looked, to Chris, maddeningly cool and fresh in spite of the heat. Chris felt she was beginning to wilt, and would have liked nothing more than to be home at Red Sands where she could have a shower and a siesta. 'I mean, it's better to be honest with each other, isn't it?' Jackie insisted. 'Burton's been so kind to me—coming to see me and making sure I have everything I need, and sending Billy and Lena to look after me. I really feel as if I have a home for the first time in my life, and someone to really care for me. Mummy always went to work and we lived in little flats and we moved so often—you can't think what it was like. Then when Mummy got married again, I felt I was really on my own. And I suppose I should clear out and move on now *you're* here and engaged to Burton and all. But I didn't know about you when I came here, and I *am* so in love with Burton. Would you like me to go, Christine? Tell me *honestly.*'

Chris felt both irritated and embarrassed. How could she ask such a stupid question after all her outpourings? Hadn't she made it very plain that she had absolutely no intention of going—that she was ready to make an all-out effort to win Burton away from Chris? Chris was beginning to think that Burton had certainly spoken the truth when he had said he had a girl on his tail. Yet it had been his idea that Jackie should come to Saltbush Flat in the first place!

She told Jackie agreeably, 'You please yourself what you

do, Jackie. It's not for me to say.'

Jackie was wide-eyed. 'You *are* a good sport, Christine! Okay then, I'll stay. I'll go on being the girl at Saltbush Flat. It's all rather fun really, isn't it?'

All in all, it had been a crazy encounter, but a very enlightening one, thought Chris later as she rode back to Red Sands. She didn't think she had acquitted herself very creditably—she certainly hadn't persuaded Jackie that it was no use putting up a fight for Burton, that he was already well and truly committed and that she would never let him go. In fact, not until she was leaving had she managed to win a single point. Then, when she was going, Jackie had paused to look at the row of wilting seedlings she had been watering in the verandah shade when Chris had arrived.

'Burton says I'll never raise them on bore water—that plants have to be well established before they'll do. But I kind of think I'm going to win out. They look a bit sick right now, but they'll perk up with a bit of attention. I was telling Burton this morning—I get up in the middle of the night sometimes to look at those seedlings and see if they want a drink. I even play records to them sometimes— plants are supposed to thrive on music, did you know that, Christine? I wish I could sing to them, but that's one thing I could never do, sing in tune.'

'What a pity,' said Chris—and maybe she did score a point there, she thought later. 'Burton plays the piano so beautifully, it's a waste if you can't sing.'

'Oh! I didn't know he played.' Jackie was quite comically taken aback. 'Can *you* sing, Christine?'

'Oh yes—I often sing in the evenings while Burton plays.'

A lie from Chris who never told lies! She wondered why she had bothered, and told herself it was because she had to make some sort of an effort on account of her bargain with Burton. But it had given her a strange feeling of pleasure to see Jackie blink those long false eyelashes of hers and be unable to find a comeback of any kind . . .

That night after dinner, Burton varied the usual routine.

He asked Chris to come and walk in the garden, and she supposed it was to give the impression to Mrs Perry and to Dan that they wanted to be alone in the moonlight. He took her arm at first, but she soon freed herself of that and there was a good foot between them as they walked slowly along the path under the scented cedar trees. Chris was wrestling with her conscience, and finally decided she must confess to Burton what she had done, so after a very few minutes she took the plunge and said awkwardly, 'You were trying to buy some place when we first met in Adelaide, weren't you, Burton? I didn't realise till today that it was Saltbush Flat.'

'Didn't you?' He sounded unsurprised. 'There would hardly have been much point in talking to you about my business affairs at that stage, Christine. You were very much wrapped up in your own sorrows. Can I take it as the first sign of recovery that you've been enquiring around the place?' He turned his face down to her, and moonlight shafting through a break in the trees made it clearly visible to her. The lines by his mouth and eyes were softened by the gentle light, and she could see the slightly sardonic curling of his lip, and feel rather than see the smouldering blue of his gaze.

Nervously, she twisted the ring on her finger and confessed determinedly, 'I wasn't enquiring around the place. I rode over to Saltbush Flat and Jackie Lester told me.'

She saw the annoyance on his face and heard it in his voice when he spoke next. 'Now what in the world did you do that for? Didn't I tell you to wait a while before you attempted that particular hurdle?'

'Not in so many words,' said Chris, standing up for herself. They were walking very slowly, and speaking in low voices. 'In fact, you were so secretive about the whole thing you can hardly blame me for feeling curious enough to do some investigating on my own account. And now I realise just why you were so close about this girl who's chasing after you.'

'Indeed.' A quick glance showed her that his eyes had

narrowed and his mouth was grim. They had reached the gate, and he leaned one hand on it and stared down at her almost menacingly. 'And why was I so close about her?'

'Because you asked her here. You could have bought Saltbush Flat, but you changed your mind so that you could ask her to come out here and stay. Maybe you didn't realise how much she was attracted to you, but I'm not in the least sorry for you——'

Now he was looking amused and incredulous. 'Is that what young Jackie told you? Well, it wasn't exactly like that, though I don't want to make a liar of the girl. Here's my version, however, Christine, and you can take your choice. I certainly did change my mind about buying Salt-bush Flat, but that was because at the last minute Jackie raised her figure more than somewhat—after all the papers had been drawn up and there was nothing left to do but sign.'

Chris said reasonably but a little triumphantly, 'If she put her price up, wouldn't that have been because she found there was oil or something on the property? I suppose she hadn't realised before what its true value was.' She stood before him, perfectly still, her head raised, and looked at him challengingly.

He said, his voice steely, 'Are you trying to tell me, Christine, that you think I'm the kind of man who would try to take advantage of a woman's ignorance? Answer me, because I really want to know.'

Chris felt a chill go down her spine. She raised one hand and nervously lifted the hair from the back of her neck, then let it slip limply and silkily down again. She hadn't intended to imply any such thing, but of course her words had implied it. No wonder he was angry. She said, 'No, of course not, Burton. I'm sorry. I just didn't think far enough ahead.'

'That would seem to be quite a habit of yours,' he said bitingly.

Her temper flared at this remark—at this autocratic acceptance of her apology and his failure to acknowledge it with at least some degree of grace. She said angrily, 'Of course *you* always think way ahead.'

'So I do,' he agreed, laconic now, and she could feel his eyes studying her.

'So you were so clever you invited Jackie here and then found you were in such a mess you had to ask me to pretend to be engaged to you.'

'Hmm,' he said measuringly. 'Let's sort out this tangle, Christine.'

Chris thought rebelliously, 'Oh, dear me, yes—he can't bear anyone to think *he*'s ever done anything rash or foolish —it's all right for me to have behaved like a ninny half my life ...' She came to stand beside him, leaning against the gate too, and said pertly, 'Yes, let's. I'm longing to hear your explanation of such a gigantic muddle, Burton.'

She saw his eyebrows go up and the angry twitch to his mouth, but after a second he said almost humouringly, 'First of all, I didn't invite Jackie Lester here, Christine. She simply told me she was coming.'

'But she said——' began Chris.

'I don't give a damn what she said, my girl. I'm telling you what happened ... I can't very well keep the girl off her own property, now can I?'

'No,' said Chris. Certainly that was reasonable enough.

'And as it is very important to me to get hold of Saltbush Flat, I don't want even to try. It would hardly be politic to tell Jackie to go to hell and to take her business elsewhere. Agreed?'

'You mean she'd find another buyer?'

'Exactly. As things stand, I'm the—*buyer*—she's interested in. And that's the way I want it. Up until now, I've been able to lease the pastures at Saltbush, but the lease has run out and Jackie, naturally enough, is not interested in renewing it. She's well aware that her new acquisition has added tremendously to her already more than adequate attractions.'

He smiled down lazily at Chris, who said stiffly, 'I see.' She wanted to ask, 'And now, do you have to go to see her every day?' But that might sound as if she cared, and she did not, she told herself. She said instead, 'Frankly, I can't see why you're so keen on Saltbush Flat. It doesn't look much of a place to me—it's no better than Red Sands, anyhow.'

'You don't like Red Sands?' he questioned, half banteringly, half seriously, but then didn't wait for her to answer. 'As for Saltbush, you haven't seen much of it, Christine. It's one of nature's freaks. Even when there are drought conditions all around—and we're on the verge of a drought right now—there are pastures there that are lush and prolific. It's valuable fattening country, and has been worth a packet to me all the years I've been leasing it from old Arthur Lester. I have buyers who come here, discriminating buyers who are particularly interested in quality and who know they'll get it from beasts with my brand on them that have been fattened on Saltbush.' He paused, and reached for her hand but failed to get possession of it as she withdrew it swiftly from the gate. 'Does that explain everything to your satisfaction?'

Chris said, 'Why don't you just give Jackie the price she wants and be done with it?'

He said dryly, 'You are a little naïve, Christine. The odds are that if I offered to do just that, there'd be another hitch. The figure might soar again, and I'm not going to be bluffed. To get down to basics, that girl is letting me know in a not particularly subtle way that there's one sure way I can get hold of Saltbush, and that's by marrying her. It may seem incomprehensible to you just now that any girl in her right mind would ever want to marry me—or would, in fact, want to marry anyone other than that vigneron who's trampled all over your heart—but Jackie Lester is very willing indeed to become my wife.'

'And that's where I come in,' said Chris with distaste. 'I'm supposed to convince her that you're not available. And supposing I do—what happens then?'

'She puts her price down to a realistic level and I buy. In any case, in a very short time she's going to discover that it's not a great deal of fun living in the outback. The bush is a lonely place, particularly at night, and I'm rather counting on that, so don't be making too many friendly calls, will you, there's a good girl.'

'And what if I don't convince her that you're not free?' Chris persisted. 'It's not going to be easy.'

He shrugged carelessly. 'Just do your best. In any case, I'm going to have that property, so don't feel overloaded with responsibility on my behalf.'

As he said that, Chris recalled what he had said about the French regarding marriage as an economic contract. She gave him a quick look, her eyes thoughtful. He certainly had the air of a man who always won his battles, and just now there was a ruthless look about his mouth. It was a mouth that could, she knew, smile very charmingly, that could soften when in repose—and she had seen it do so sometimes when he played the piano—into lines that reminded her of the lips of Greek statues she had seen in pictures. It was a mouth whose curves were slightly sensual and there was a deep indentation at one corner that made his smile a little off balance and therefore rather fascinating ... She gave a start as he said, 'It's really a great pity you took it upon yourself to go traipsing over there today without my permission, Christine. I wanted to put it off till I felt you were ready to give a convincing performance of an engaged girl.'

Chris flushed. 'You should have told me your plans. And I'm sorry, but I don't think I'll ever be able to come up to your expectations.'

'We'll have to give you some intensive training,' he said, with a slight smile. She saw his eyes go to her mouth, and thought instantly, 'He's going to kiss me.' She felt herself tense, and then he said dryly, 'Meanwhile, you might try a bit harder. We did make a bargain, you know.' He took her arm firmly. 'Now come along, it must be past your bedtime.'

It was, somehow, an anticlimax.

CHAPTER FOUR

So now Chris had it quite plainly. She was being used to strike a bargain—to enable Burton Alexander to get hold of Saltbush Flat at a price he was prepared to pay. How prosaic it was! But Chris had a notion that Burton was really up against some opposition. Jackie Lester was little and cute and doll-like, but she was determined too, she had her own plans, and in Chris's book, it was well and truly in the odds that Burton would eventually marry her—if only as an economic proposition!

'Well,' thought Chris, 'it's not my business if it ends that way.' Yet a feeling that she had some responsibility irked her. It irked her too that she must be so passive. Now that she knew the set-up, she longed to be up and doing, to bring the whole thing to a head, one way or another. She felt more restless than ever about staying around the homestead. She took rides, swam at the waterhole, tried to make friends with Jason, played with the small aboriginal children. And each afternoon she rested on the lounger on the side verandah, trying to get through the most enervating period of the day. The air was oppressive with heat then, and the tamarisks and cedars that lined the path were utterly motionless. Not a thing moved. The aboriginal girls went over the yard to their own quarters, and Mrs Perry rested in her sitting room. Sometimes there was the sound of a motor as Joe or the two stockmen who worked around the homestead tinkered with machinery that needed attention. And always there was the monotonous sound of the pump engine at the main windmill near the homestead—a sound so constant that after a while one scarcely heard it.

Late one afternoon she went into the garden for some fresh air and encountered Mrs Perry, vigorously clipping yellow jasmine flowers to make a table decoration. She gave

70

a visible start of surprise when Chris spoke to her, and said apologetically, 'I must look as though I'm chopping heads off, and I suppose in a way I am. Fact is, I get so upset when I think about Saltbush. When Arthur Lester was alive it was just as if it were another part of the Red Sands run. I always thought Arthur would leave it to Burton. He was in and out of my kitchen here as if he were family ... And now there's all this business of moving the cattle back to pastures that are all but eaten out already. They'll be skin and bone, and not fit to sell, those cattle will.' She snipped a few more sprays and put them in her basket. 'There, that's about enough and something left over for the bedrooms ... *Paddy* says Burton could put it all straight tomorrow if he wanted,' she added darkly. 'But I don't see how, I really don't.'

'I see how,' thought Chris to herself. But she wondered why *Paddy* should say Burton could set it all straight. Did Paddy know the truth about Chris—a truth that no one else knew? Did *he* know that there was no engagement to break, no love to be denied?

Later, she thought about that land that Burton wanted so badly and wished that she could see it. She decided that, despite his orders, she would ride over to Saltbush again. She was curious to see Jackie again, and maybe, too, she was spoiling for a fight! Burton never bothered to pass on any information, and she found his incommunicativeness aggravating. One night, after they had gone on to the verandah, she burst out, 'You never tell me about anything, Burton. I'm just stuck here all day and you're out on the run and—and everywhere——'

He gave her a look that was vastly amused. 'You sound like an aggrieved wife, Christine. I don't ask about *your* day, do I? And if I don't talk, it's because I respect your privacy and don't want to interrupt all the thoughts that must be busily racing around in your head.'

'*What* thoughts?' Chris asked aggressively, sure that he was going to make some slighting reference to Francis, and realising with some surprise that her moodiness and constant feeling of incredulous grief about Francis's behaviour had tapered off considerably since she had come to Red Sands.

But instead of referring to Francis, Burton said sardonically, 'Well, aren't you planning out a new future for yourself? Deciding what kind of a career you'll take up when you leave Red Sands and my protection?'

Chris looked at him blankly, almost open-mouthed. She hadn't given her career a thought!

'Well?' he repeated. 'Surely your convalescence has progressed far enough for you to have *some* ideas. I can't imagine that you'll want to stay in the outback for ever, putting up with the heat and the loneliness.'

'*You* stay here,' said Chris perversely. 'So does Mrs Perry—and——'

He nodded, his profile towards her. 'It's tolerable to some people—more than tolerable to a few. To me, it's the only life. I couldn't live anywhere else. But I was born here. You're not really an outback girl, are you? ... By the way, I meant to tell you that Peg Spencer is coming home— she'll be here tomorrow. Poor girl, she'd far rather Dan had a job closer to the city. I guess I'll have to find myself a new book-keeper shortly—pity he hadn't chosen his life's partner with a bit more care. However, let's get back to you and your future and hear *your* thoughts.'

Chris twisted the ring on her finger and stood up restlessly. She went to stand at the verandah rail and looked out into the warm darkness of the night. She could smell the yellow jasmine and the little mauve cedar flowers and was aware of a strange melting feeling in her bones. It was beautiful here. Crazily, starkly beautiful, and it was taking a hold of her. The midday heat might sometimes be almost unbearable, but other things made up for that—the beauty and bigness of the night sky for one.

Burton came to stand beside her.

'What a night!' he said softly. 'Stars and jasmine and the soft, soft air. All we need now is a little music and a little loving.'

His tone unnerved her strangely—made her aware of her heart again. Not of its pain, but of its vulnerability. She moved to the steps and walked down into the garden as though in a dream, and again Burton followed her. They took the path through the gate crossed the gravel yard in silence, passed the saddle store and hay shed and came to the horse yards.

There was only a slip of a moon, but the stars were bright and their shadows moved black and sharp on the ground. One or two lights shone from the stockmen's quarters, and there was a distant light from Mrs Perry's end of the homestead. No music, no love ... Chris stole a look at Burton's face and found he was studying her.

'What are you thinking about, Christine?' His voice was warm, almost caressing, and he was very close to her.

Chris said rashly, 'Love.'

'Love.' He repeated the word thoughtfully. Then after a second he said briskly, 'Have you taken Sally out lately? I believe you enjoy riding.'

'Yes, I've been out, but not far. I think I'll ride over to Saltbush Flat tomorrow,' said Chris in a rush. She had more or less made up her mind about that, but she hadn't really intended telling Burton.

'You must be in the mood for putting on a good show, then,' he commented.

'What do you mean, a good show?'

'Come now—you know perfectly well what I mean, my little fiancée,' he said banteringly.

Chris turned her head aside. 'I simply thought I'd call to see how Jackie's getting on,' she said scathingly.

'She's getting on fine. She's up to her ears in home decorating. She's going to paint every room in that house, and then she's going to make a stack of curtains. Such are her plans—though I doubt if she'll complete them. Don't worry, Christine, I'm keeping an eye on young Jackie.'

Chris said swiftly, her eyes glinting, 'I hope *you're* putting on a good show, Burton.'

He cocked his eyebrows and considered that for a moment. 'That's a good line,' he said then. 'The touch of jealousy ... But never fear, when I visit Jackie, I'm as innocent as Red Riding Hood taking a basket of goodies to Granny.'

Chris had to smile wryly at the image he called up, but she wondered, all the same.

'What I was going to suggest,' continued Burton after a moment, 'was that you should skip the social call tomorrow and——'

'And *what*? Must I have your permission for everything I do?'

'Certainly not. But you might wait for me to finish what I was saying. I was about to suggest, that if you care to, you can come up in the plane with me tomorrow. I want to cast an eye over Saltbush Flat to see if we've made a proper job of the muster, and then I want to take a look at a few patches of possible feed. So what do you say? Would you like to come?'

Christine felt a surge of excitement. 'I'd like it very much,' she said eagerly.

'Fine. Then for a change we might breakfast together—not too early—and leave straight afterwards. Okay?'

'Yes,' said Chris. And added, 'Thank you.'

'My pleasure,' he said gravely.

Chris enjoyed herself the next morning more than she had done in a long time. It gave her a terrific kick to be flying over this great cattle property on the edge of the desert. She had been tight with inner tension on the flight up from Adelaide, and Francis's treachery had still been apt to take over her mind and make her moody and depressed. Now her usual lively personality was beginning to assert itself. Perhaps it had even been stimulating to have a few arguments with Burton, to find in his attitude to her something to kick against!

They took off smoothly from the small airstrip and climbed gently into the sunny blue of the sky. Then Burton brought the aircraft round in a wide turn and headed for the

Saltbush Flat property. A warm wind lifted Chris's red hair to fly, a bright red flag, behind her. Today she had caught it to one side and tied it with a chiffon scarf that matched the coral blouse she wore with her sand-coloured pants. Burton had complimented her on her appearance at breakfast.

'I'd never have picked on that colour for a redhead, but my oh my, it surely does something for Christine, doesn't it, Mrs Perry?'

Mrs Perry had agreed that it did, and as he left the table, Burton had given Chris's hair a playful tug that had brought colour to her cheeks and confusion to her mind. Now, sitting beside him in the plane, she looked down to see the receding cluster of buildings on Red Sands. All around was a desert landscape, flat and bare and red, the thin covering of mulga and saltbush and spinifex minimised by distance.

'Beginning to look familiar?' asked Burton conversationally. 'I suppose you know the mulga, Christine. It's an acacia—a desert tree that's adapted itself to its environment with its stocky leaf stalks and undeveloped leaf blade that reduces water loss. Trees are like people. Either they thrive in a particular environment, or they die—though with people, it may be only a metaphorical death ... I had a talk to Dan earlier on this morning, and he's going to tell Peg that they'll leave the outback.'

'Oh, poor Dan!' exclaimed Chris involuntarily. 'Does Peg hate it so much?' She turned from her scrutiny of the reds and grey-greens of the earth below to look enquiringly at Burton.

'I'm afraid she does.'

'But Dan's here—and she has her children. I should think she could be happy at Red Sands.'

'Really? I didn't know you had such thoughts ... Look down in five minutes, Christine, and you'll see something really worth looking at.'

Chris saw what he meant exactly five minutes later. First, she saw the line of a fence, like a thin wavering pencil line—the fence that divided Red Sands from Saltbush Flat. Then she saw the bungalow where Jackie Lester lived, and its huddle of neglected outhouses. All around she saw the red earth, she saw where bores had been sunk, and she saw the deep slits that were dry creek beds. And then, suddenly, like a mirage that turned out to be real and no mirage all, she saw the deep rich green of grass, the bright sheen of water, clumps of shady trees. Pastures that were spread out lavishly, pastures that went on and on.

She let out a little gasp and leaned from the plane to take it in the better. All that rich, verdant land! It was unbelievable! No wonder Burton wanted Saltbush Flat!

And then suddenly it all came to an end—as definitely as though the earth had been stripped bare beyond it. Once again there was only mulga dotted on a red, sunbaked background. And far out on that red plain was a great mob of cattle, enveloped in a rising, restless dust haze. A few stockmen on horses circled it as it moved slowly, fractionally, inch by inch it seemed, over the dusty dried-up ground, away from the rich green fodder in its remarkable outcrop in the midst of the desert.

'Those are our prize beasts,' Burton said grimly. 'Picked for sale, brought here to fatten. Paddy's taking them back to feed at the Long Bore on Red Sands for a start. I want to check that we've cleared them all out of the scrub.'

He brought the plane down low then, and skimmed over the ground, watching intently. Chris could see clearly the line of the fence that enclosed Saltbush Flat. Inside was the long, long stretch of red plain and that lesser rectangle of green. Nothing more. She asked in surprise, 'Is that all of Saltbush Flat?'

'Every bit of it,' he admitted wryly. 'It's merely a strip half way along this side of my run. But what a strip! Once it belonged to the Alexanders. I'll tell you the story one day, Christine, if you're interested ... Right now, we're going to head north and take a look at the feed around one or two of the waterholes. I've a bit of hard thinking ahead of me. I don't want my picked stock to lose too much condition, and hence I don't want to move them further than is absolutely necessary. And believe me, I'll get them back on those Saltbush pastures very shortly, though I have to perjure my soul to do it.'

He spoke forcefully and Chris looked at him with trepidation. She was struck anew by his vastly masculine good looks, and though his sun-streaked hair, tousled by the wind, gave him an oddly carefree appearance, yet his face was hard and his brows drawn darkly. She wondered exactly what he meant when he said, 'Though I have to perjure my soul to do it.' Could he be referring to the possibility of marrying Jackie Lester?

She remarked caustically, 'What a pity you didn't buy Saltbush Flat from Jackie's uncle years ago, Burton. That way, you'd have had no problems. I presume as he leased out his pastures, he wasn't all that keen on owning them.'

He gave her a sardonic look. 'Christine, you're ignorant on so many counts you'd do better not to express an opinion.'

'Well, I'm not the sort of girl to sit still and say nothing, whether you like it or not,' flashed Chris, stung by his criticism. 'And if I'm so ignorant it's because you've kept me so—even though I'm supposed to be your fiancée.'

'Then we'll remedy that. To begin with, Arthur Lester wasn't Jackie's uncle. He was her father's second cousin. And I offered to buy Saltbush not once, but many times. But Arthur was an eccentric old bloke. He'd have been lost without Saltbush Flat. He refused to sell it because he was stuck with a dream—a lifelong dream that never came true. One day, he was going to strike oil, or maybe nickel or lithium or vermiculite or what have you, on that land of his. Hence all the bores, none of which ever produced anything more than water.'

'Oh,' exclaimed Chris, 'but Jackie said——'

'All Jackie knows about Arthur and what he found or didn't find,' said Burton, 'is what she heard repeated by some of his old scallywags of friends who were at the funeral. She and her mother hadn't set eyes on the old fellow since Jackie was a cute four-year-old . . . No, Christine. Saltbush's treasure lies solely in its pastures.'

He said nothing more for some time, and Chris, though she did not feel exactly chastened, admitted to herself that she had certainly been ignorant of a few salient facts. Jackie had given her to understand quite plainly that she had known her 'Uncle' Arthur well, and been very fond of him.

She looked down from the plane, knowing that Burton was now assessing possible feeding places for his sale cattle. It seemed remarkable to her that cattle could live and thrive on land that looked so barren from the air. Bores and well-filled dams showed up abundantly, but the feed looked scanty and dried out, and it was clear that good, drenching rain was badly needed. Here and there, cattled moved, no bigger than toys, hazed by dust, and then, as Burton turned the aircraft, Chris thought she spotted the ruins of some old stone house standing in the midst of a wasteland.

'What's that down there, Burton?' she asked curiously, and he paused for a moment before he answered her.

'That's the old Red Sands homestead, Christine.'

Chris stared. '*There?*' she asked incredulously. She could see no water, next to no vegetation apart from a bit of mulga, and not far distant was a fantastic landscape of red sandhills, running parallel with each other and seeming to extend to eternity, like the great red waves of a petrified and endless sea. She felt herself shiver. 'Why would anyone ever build out there?'

'I'll take you out some time and tell you all about it,' said Burton. His voice had a strange note in it, a note of remoteness and austerity that Chris had never heard before, and for a time it kept her silent. Then, when they were once more over familiar territory, she said, 'I should like to hear about Red Sands, Burton.'

He cocked an eyebrow at her. 'Would you? Are you really interested in the Alexander family, Christine? Or do you see it as—part of your job?'

'I'm human—and as curious as anyone else,' said Chris, feeling rebuffed.

'So you're curious. I wonder is that a healthy sign? Are you quite sure that family histories won't interfere with your grief?'

She bit her lip. 'I'm just a little tired of your gibes, Burton. Can't I be treated as a normal girl?'

'Well—*can* you, Christine? I should very much like to think that you could. Maybe we'll conduct a little experiment tonight.'

If she had imagined that he would relate family history to her that night, she was quite wrong. His experiment took another form altogether, and came when she rose from her chair on the verandah to say goodnight. Burton rose too, and said in his usual pleasant way, 'Goodnight, Christine, I hope you enjoyed your day.'

'I did,' said Chris. 'Thank you for taking me with you.'

'We must do it again some time.' Almost without her being aware of it, he had taken her by the hand, and now with a quick jerk he pulled her into his arms and kissed her. Christine struggled mainly because of the unexpectedness of it, and abruptly he let her go and told her callously, 'So now we know how much of a normal girl you are, Christine. You're stuck well and truly in the past. Today isn't real to you. It's all yesterday. The only kisses you can tolerate are dream kisses—repeats of past performances of your unfaithful vigneron.'

Chris was breathing fast. 'Let me tell you this, Burton Alexander—I didn't know *this* sort of thing was included in our—our arrangement.'

'No? You thought we could act the part of a couple in love and never even touch one another?'

'I didn't think at all,' said Chris. 'If I had, I'd never have come here.'

'You'd have stayed neck deep in your bath of adolescent self-pity, and finally allowed yourself to be packed off to secretarial school. Well, it would have served you right.'

'I'd have got a job in the bush,' retorted Chris, smarting. 'I'm not all that helpless.'

'I'm glad to hear it. But I can't imagine any sort of job

you'd have been fit for, in *your* mental and emotional state. At any rate, now you're here, what do you intend to do about it? For believe me, I shan't make it easy for you to go.'

'I'm sure you shan't,' snapped Chris. 'So I'll make the best of it, that's all.' She had reached the house door now. 'But not for any longer than I can help. I promise you ...'

'Almost as if to defy him, she rode out to Saltbush Flat the next day, and this time she was on her mettle. To a degree, she thought it would serve Burton right if he had to marry Jackie Lester to get what he wanted, and yet it mightn't be such a terrible penance really. Jackie had quite a few points in her favour, and she was certainly industrious. Since Chris had last seen her, she had finished painting the sitting room, and now it was a marvel with its pretty off-white walls and green skirting boards. Her seedlings were still alive, and when Chris arrived she was on the verandah measuring curtain lengths from some orange stuff.

'Hello,' she greeted Chris with a smile. 'How gorgeous to see you! Burton said you might come in, and I hoped you would. I love company even when I'm busy ... What do you think of this material? It's not exactly what I wanted—a bit too cottagy, don't you think?—but it's a terrific colour. Burton thinks it would look fab in the sitting room, and so do I.'

'Then it hardly matters what *I* think, does it?' said Chris, who was feeling hot and dusty and thirsty. Jackie looked the essence of coolness in pale blue today, her legs bare, her feet thrust into sketchy white sandals. Looking at her, Chris couldn't help reflecting that however detachedly Burton talked about the girl at Saltbush Flat, he couldn't help being aware of her little girl prettiness.

Jackie was pouting. 'You mustn't be *jealous*, Christine. You do see a lot more of Burton than I do, you know ... Anyhow, sit down for a moment. I just want to finish cutting this or I'll forget all my measurements. Then we'll have a cool drink, because you *do* look so hot and thirsty.'

Chris was hardly mollified, but she sat down and studied

Jackie cautiously. She didn't look like a girl who was racked by loneliness, who was on the point of running off to civilisation and crowds. She seemed remarkably happy, remarkably well adjusted, and now and again she sang rather tunelessly as she measured and snipped.

She asked after a moment, 'What's your background, Christine? Do you have a rich family or something? Burton never says much and I *am* curious.'

Chris said dryly, 'Yes—I do have a rich family.'

'Then that's why Burton is thinking of marrying you. Isn't it?' she added with a guileless widening of her blue eyes that infuriated Chris. How rude could you be!

'Sorry—you're completely wrong,' Chris said coldly, and that at least was true.

'Have you decided on a date for the wedding?'

'Not yet.' Chris began to wonder why she had come after all. It seemed it was to be interrogated by Jackie Lester, and made to feel uncomfortable, and that did not suit her at all. She decided that attack was the only answer to Jackie's tactics...

'No plans!' said Jackie, looking very well satisfied.

'Not yet,' said Chris firmly, and changed direction. 'Aren't you scared here all alone most of the day and night?'

'Not a bit!' Jackie looked surprised at such a suggestion. She drew the scissors not very expertly through the orange material, and Chris thought, 'She's going to have problems getting *that* to hang straight.' It was woven crooked, and looked rather cheap material. 'After all, I've got Lena and Billy—Burton insisted on that. And then *he* comes to see me every single day, and now *you're* here. Would you be lonely, Christine? If you would, then I don't think you should marry Burton, I really don't ... I'm not like that. I just love this place. I guess I look on it as my home now. I don't think I'll ever want to leave here.'

'You won't want to sell?'

Jackie shrugged, and folded her material. 'It's great here ... What's it like at Red Sands homestead, Christine? I bet it's a place that needs a woman's touch.'

'It has a woman's touch,' said Chris.

'Oh, you mean the housekeeper! What's she like?'

'Very nice and very competent,' said Chris. She could sense that Jackie was immensely curious about Red Sands, and was probably breaking her neck to get there. And Burton hadn't invited her. Well, that was something!

'Burton will take me over one day,' said Jackie comfortably. 'Now that he knows you and I are such good friends.' She gave Chris a quick look from beneath her long lashes and Chris smiled a little.

'I shouldn't count on it, Jackie … Did you see us flying over here yesterday morning?'

The other girl looked slightly disconcerted. 'Were you up in that plane, Christine? I don't think I'd like it much—it's such a silly little contraption.'

'Better not tell Burton that,' warned Chris. 'It wouldn't do your stock any good at all.'

Jackie eyed her suspiciously and suddenly smiled. 'You *are* taking it all in good part, Christine! I was scared you were getting really cranky.'

When Chris finally rode away she warned herself, 'Don't go there again. You just can't win.'

Now that Peg Spencer was back at Red Sands, Dan had dinner in his own bungalow, and Chris was more thankful than ever for Mrs Perry's presence at the dinner table. She and Burton had scarcely exchanged a word since the other evening, and even their after-dinner sessions had come to an end, for Burton seemed to have business that took him to the office every night. Chris began to have a notion of how lonely one could be out here, and to wish that Frith would come. She went to visit Peg Spencer once or twice, but she was a querulous young woman, continually fussing over her two small children and making complaints over a bungalow that seemed to Chris to contain every comfort that one could wish for. She felt sorry for Dan, whom she liked very much.

She felt a little sorry for herself too, and wished very much that Burton would hold out the olive branch.

Then unexpectedly she came out to breakfast one morning to find he had not yet gone out on the run. He had just risen from the breakfast table, and he stuck his thumbs in his narrow snakeskin belt and looked at her consideringly.

'How is Christine this morning? Mrs Perry thinks you've been fretting while I've been locked up in the office working. But believe me, it's been necessary ... Would you like a day out with me today, Christine?'

He spoke banteringly, but though there was a smile on his lips, Chris thought there was a watchfulness at the back of those oddly soft, hyacinth-blue eyes. But he was—surely he was—extending the olive branch, and she was surprised at how gladly and eagerly she grasped it.

'I'd love it, Burton.'

'You would?' He raked his fingers through his thick hair, and one bleached lock fell tantalisingly across his forehead. Chris felt her heart lurch and tried not to notice it. 'Famous last words, my girl—I'm going out to the edge of the desert, and it's going to be mighty hot ... However, eat up your breakfast.' He turned to Mrs Perry briefly. 'Better see she's well sustained, old dear ... Then fetch your hat, Christine, and tie up that long hair of yours. Meanwhile, I'll get Joe to check over the jeep.'

He disappeared and Chris sat down to eat her breakfast —steak with two eggs, toast and a pot of tea. The sun was already striking fiercely through the vines that shaded this end of the verandah, and she reflected that it would certainly be hot by midday. Mrs Perry, who had been hovering over her attentively, sat down opposite her as she poured herself a final cup of tea, and said slowly, 'Don't be upset by anything you see or hear today, will you, Christine? You love Burton, don't you?'

That seemed to Chris quite unanswerable and a slow flush mounted to her cheeks and ebbed away.

Mrs Perry said after a moment, 'You're a fine girl, Christine. I like you very much. And I want Burton to be happy. Believe me, he's one of the best men you could hope to meet in a lifetime—a man you could trust with your very soul. If he makes you his wife, Christine, then he'll look after you till his dying day. Remember that, won't you, love?'

It was a strange little speech, and while it warmed Chris's heart that Mrs Perry should call her 'love' so affectionately, she felt vaguely apprehensive.

What did the housekeeper think she might hear or see today that could upset her?

She discovered the answer to that question, but not till much later in the day.

It was a day that started like a picnic and ended in confusion.

'You'll have a real taste of the outback today, Christine,' Burton told her as he helped her into the jeep. He was pleasant and kind, and there seemed to be a truce between them as they drove over the plain and he pointed out various types of acacias and eucalypts, and named different wild flowers that Chris did not know. She felt herself lulled and entertained, and instructed as well, as the long heat of the morning passed. They lunched in the shade of a grove of trees with pretty grey-green foliage, that grew by a long, deeply green waterhole lying in a cleft in the red rocky ground. There were no cattle tracks here, but small birds came fearlessly to flirt with their reflections, white butterflies drifted about, and dragonflies with shimmering wings of red and green and blue skimmed over the tranquil water. It was an unexpectedly beautiful little spot, and Chris loved it, and said so as she laid out the cold beef, the crisp lettuce and tomatoes, and the pretty potato salad sprinkled with mint, that Mrs Perry had provided.

'Eden Lake,' said Burton, settling himself comfortably on a cotton rug on the ground and letting her wait on him. 'All that's left of the Garden of Eden that once lay all across the plain beyond. Make the most of the shade and prettiness, Christine, because that plain is now the worst stretch of country on this run, and that's where we're going when we've eaten.'

In spite of his warning, Chris was appalled by what she saw not much later—a bare merciless desert, with the odd clump of spinifex, the odd stretch of stunted mulga. A desert that glittered and burned with unrelieved heat. High in the sky, eagle hawks glided, birds of the sun, light flashing off their wings as they wheeled, so that they looked like flakes of dark sinister metal stripped from the burnished steel of the sky.

Burton, driving slowly but confidently over stony ground where no tracks lay, told her, 'When my grandfather bought this stretch of land many years ago it was beautiful cattle country, covered in rich green feed.'

'I can't believe it,' breathed Chris. She could feel the heat striking up from the ground like fire, and her whole body was burningly hot. 'It's terrible—a terrible land.' She could hear the harsh cawing of crows that were nowhere to be seen, and she wondered if they were real or had been called up by her imagination as the natural inhabitants of this stark relentless landscape.

'Yes, it's terrible,' Burton agreed. 'My grandfather was a wealthy cattleman when he expanded up here. He'd travelled all over this part of the country, and the feed here —like that on Saltbush which was then part of the Alexander property—was more than somewhat of a miracle. He bought it, and in a fit of mistaken generosity proceeded to make over Saltbush to his unmarried sister. Great-Aunt Grace, though well into her fifties, was then very smartly snapped up by a widower, with a grown-up son, Arthur.'

Chris blinked. 'Arthur Lester?'

'The same.'

'Well,' said Chris, 'you'd understand *that*, Burton.'

'I'd understand what?'

'That marriage. Arthur's father,' said Chris carefully, 'obviously looked on marriage as an economic proposition. Isn't that how you put it? Very sensible of him. I don't think your Great-Aunt Grace was to blame at all.'

'Did I say she was?' he asked equably. 'The initial mistake was my grandfather's. Just as, in this present set-up, the mistake is Arthur Lester's. In my view, women should never be made land-holders.'

'Then you don't think your sister should have a share in Red Sands?'

His mouth tightened. 'I don't. And she hasn't.'

'That's not fair!'

'It's very fair. It's a protection for Frith.'

'So no one will marry her for her property?'

'Exactly. Frith would make a very desirable wife for an outback man if she were part owner of Red Sands.'

'And you don't want to share your inheritance?' Chris didn't know what drove her on to rudeness, but she seemed to get a sort of satisfaction out of sparring with Burton.

'Is that what you think of me, Christine?' he asked quizzically. 'Well, you can look at it that way if you like, but while you're condemning me you might remember it was my father who arranged things this way. He didn't want—and I don't want—to see Frith married to a cattleman. If it's my comfort to you, she does have a nice little packet of shares that means she doesn't have to work unless she wants to.'

Chris digested this in silence. She wondered a little about those shares. Burton hadn't said his *father* had given them to Frith. She glanced at him quickly. Had *he* made the gift to Frith because his father had left her nothing? And why was it neither of them wanted Frith to marry a cattleman?

Burton said after a brief silence, 'Now let me finish telling you about this Eden that mysteriously and steadily degenerated into a desert. Can you imagine how it happened, Christine?'

Chris, pushing back a stray lock of hair from her neck, shook her head.

'Witchcraft,' said Burton. She stared at him open-mouthed to see if he was joking, but he looked perfectly serious. His eyes were on that non-existent track and he was intent on avoiding the larger boulders. 'These were the sacred hunting grounds of the Wingealla tribe, Christine—

long before the white man came here. They deeply resented the intrusion of the Alexanders, and while it can't be said they actually killed the old man, still they pointed the bone at him. Any stock that grazed here was stricken by an unidentifiable and fatal disease. The pastures, once eaten out, refused to renew themselves. The waterholes dried up, and, contrary to all scientific evidence, not a single bore that was ever sunk tapped water. The old man's heart was broken quite literally, I think, to see his kingdom disintegrating about him. My father had to take over and to work like ten men, with Saltbush Flat gone and this great plain useless.'

Chris was silent, finding the story more than a little eerie. Suddenly she had the feeling that a group of stunted twisted trees they were passing were dark-skinned, hostile warriors—watching them. And when a flock of black cockatoos flew into the air like cinders from a dead fire caught in a whirlwind, shrieking in a devilish way, she let out an audible gasp of fear.

'Frightened, Christine?' Burton asked laconically. 'It's a hostile, incomprehensible land—is that what you're thinking?'

'Maybe I am,' said Chris soberly. 'I'm glad I wasn't around when your grandfather came here.'

'I'm glad you weren't too,' said Burton, and flashed her a smile—one of his slightly crooked, fascinating smiles. 'I'd far rather you were here right now.'

His smile and his words did something so drastic to Chris's heart it frightened her almost more than his story. She said quickly, acidly, 'Because you want to use me when you're bargaining to get Saltbush Flat?'

He shrugged. 'Maybe. But also because I like your red hair and that fiery temper of yours that flares up at times and assures me you've a great deal of life and spirit hiding behind those great sad grey eyes of yours, Christine.'

Still further disconcerted, Chris could not look at him. She looked, instead, straight ahead of her, and gave a small start of surprise as she saw the ruins of the house they had seen the other day from the air. As the jeep drew nearer, a hot wind blew towards them like a wind blowing off fire, and heat haze shook violently over the shambles of the ragged roofless walls that had once enclosed a home. The old Alexander home.

Presently Burton pulled up and they both sat in silence. 'Want to take a look, Christine?' He was staring with a bleak expression ahead of him, and she felt herself shiver.

'Did *you* ever live here, Burton?'

'Yes. When I was a child. They were hard times then. This was a huge holding but an almost bankrupt one. The stock had dwindled and lost quality, and we went through five hard years of drought. That's how it can be in the outback, Christine. You can take nothing for granted. My father worked harder than you can possibly imagine, with no money to restock or build fences or sink bores, and with only a few aboriginal stockmen to help him—and *they* were likely to go walkabout at any tick of the clock. Another tragedy—my mother was killed while riding when I was a very small child——'

Chris asked quickly, 'Frith?'

'Frith is my stepsister. My father married again when I was away at school. Things had improved—financially—when he brought Amy here as a bride. She was a beautiful talented girl of twenty-two. You must have seen her portrait at home. Father still had to be out on the run for weeks at a time, and she, poor girl, went out of her mind with loneliness and despair. One day when her baby was no more than a few weeks old she walked out into the sandhills and simply disappeared.'

He told the story starkly, sketchily, and Chris thought with deep compassion of that lovely young girl with the ethereal features and the slightly untilted eyes whose life had ended in tragedy.

Abruptly, Burton climbed out of the jeep. 'Come along, Christine.' He began to walk with a sort of restlessness towards the ruins that had once been his home, and Chris followed in silence. He said over his shoulder, 'My father believed that both the women he loved were destroyed by witchcraft—that there was a curse on the Alexanders. We left here after Amy disappeared and lived in what was little more than a hut until the new homestead was built. Unfortunately my father died before Arthur Lester decided to give up running cattle—a business which he'd never either like or understood—and I was able to lease Saltbush Flat and restore our—kingdom—to its original splendour. And now, by heaven, I'm going to have those pastures back again. That's one thing for sure.'

He stepped, as he spoke, through a crumbling doorway, drawing Chris with him. In the shadows of this floorless, roofless shell, where the red sand blew and the wind as it destroyed made a sound like ghostly voices moaning, it seemed suddenly cold. But it was not a physical cold. It was a coldness of the spirit, and Chris hung back, reluctant to go further. This old house was blowing away into the nothingness of a desert landscape, and to her an aura of witchcraft seemed to hang about it. She thought of those two young women whom Burton's father believed had been taken from him by native sorcery, and she wondered if Burton believed it too. She half turned to him, a question forming on her lips, but before she could utter it he said grimly, 'It's a very serious thing to bring a woman to the outback to live, Christine. Frith is her mother's daughter—sensitive, artistic, nervy. She is never to be claimed by the outback. My father swore this to me when I was eighteen years old and he told me the truth about Amy's death.'

His hand touched her bare forearm, and his fingers were cold. At her feet, among the rubble, she saw a cluster of small red flowers, prickly, defiant, very much alive, and for some reason she touched her red hair and as she did so, caught the glint of the ruby on her finger.

'Come,' Burton said, and they both turned their backs on the shadow and destruction of the old homestead and went out once more into the bright and burning sunlight. 'What do you think, Christine? Would *you* marry me knowing there's possibly a ready-made curse waiting to fall on the shoulders of any girl I love?'

Chris felt both startled and bewildered. She was not the girl he loved, and he had never asked her to marry him. Her thoughts went fleetingly to Jackie, and she was certain *that* imperturbable girl would not be in the least concerned about witchcraft. As for herself—Chris didn't know. She had been aware of some very spine-chilling feelings as she had stood among those ruins and those ghosts.

She said, aiming for a light touch, 'You certainly have a problem there, Burton.'

'I certainly have,' he agreed after a moment. They had reached the jeep and as Chris climbed in he put a hand to his brow to shade his eyes, and stared intently across the plain. Chris glanced up, and for a while her eyes lingered on that handsome masculine face, and those blue eyes. Then his gold-tipped lashes flicked down and his eyes were looking into hers.

'See that drift of smoke away out there? I'll stake my life it's from an aborigine's fire.' His nostrils dilated subtly. 'Cooking their evening meal. Honey possum, by the smell of it. Shall we drive over and see, Christine?'

Chris bit her lip nervously. 'Would they be—aboriginals from the Wingealla tribe, Burton?'

'Quite likely,' he said casually. He strolled round the jeep and got into the driver's seat. 'That tribe's dying out, Christine, but there are still a few of them wandering around and linking up now and again with relatives who work on the cattle runs hereabouts.'

'And *do* they still hold it against you that your grandfather took away their sacred hunting grounds?' She asked the question hopefully, because she had suddenly remembered Mrs Perry saying, 'Don't be upset by anything you may see or hear.'

'I believe I've really got you worried, Christine,' Burton said. 'I have no fears about the Wingeallas. I made friends among the aborigines when I came home to Red Sands from school. I could show you a sacred cave here that no other white man has ever seen, to the best of my knowledge.'

'Could you? Is it far away?' Chris asked eagerly. She thought that she would rather visit a sacred cave any day than call on the members of a tribe that had brought such disaster and tragedy to Burton's family.

'Not far at all,' said Burton. 'We could be there in ten minutes.'

He started up the motor and Chris breathed a sigh of relief.

CHAPTER FIVE

IT was the Cave of the Winds that he showed her presently. An underground cave, its opening screened by mulga, a narrow cleft in a great slab of red rock leading steeply down to a wide, sandy-floored cavern, cool and dark. Burton flicked on the small torch he carried with him to light up the wall that was decorated with primitive drawings in ochre and red and black. There were kangaroos and emus and lizards, there were men running, men throwing spears. They were weird and fascinating X-ray-type drawings, and though Chris had seen similar pictures in books, she found that to see the actual drawings, particularly in a hidden place like this, was more than a little awesome. Her spine prickled faintly with the fear that she was on territory forbidden to women—particularly to white women!—and that if she were discovered here by a man of the Wingealla tribe, something terrible might befall her.

'You're jittery, Christine,' said Burton. 'Why? Nothing will happen to you. The men who showed me this cave are my friends, and because you're with me, you're protected.'

She glanced at him in the torchlight and saw that he was quite serious, and she knew that he had some deep feeling about this cave and about the aborigines that she couldn't yet understand. It was a glimpse of another side of his character—a mystic side. He switched off his torch and put his arm around her shoulders as they went outside again, and there, after a few paces, she drew away from him and began to walk ahead of him back to the jeep. She was uncertain what she felt, but she had a strong suspicion that it was a great deal more than *he* felt. Under those circumstances, she didn't want his arm laid caressingly across her shoulders.

Suddenly, as she walked ahead of him, her hand flew to her mouth and she stood stock-still, paralysed with fright. A great lizard, some five feet tall, looking like a prehistoric monster, was running full tilt towards her on its hind legs. It was as though one of those fantastic drawings in the cave had come to life and was chasing her, and the thought of witchcraft sprang into her mind and shook her to the foundations.

Then she felt Burton's arms close around her from behind, just a second before the goanna swerved aside and clawed its way rapidly up a tree. Chris pressed her face to Burton's breast and shuddered against him.

'It's only a goanna, sweetheart,' he comforted her, laughing a little. 'Haven't you ever met a goanna face to face before?'

'Never,' breathed Chris, feeling a shameful coward, for of course she would have come to no harm. But she stayed where she was for another five seconds and then felt sufficiently composed to draw away. She looked up at him and felt herself netted in his blue stare—like an insect. 'His eyes,' she thought suddenly, 'give nothing away. Their colour is so benign and god-like and enchanting—so Elysian. But what is hidden behind them? What is he thinking?' For a long moment she stared back at him, trying to read what was in his mind. Did he believe even a little in witchcraft? Or was he almost wholly materialistic—so much so that he would act quite cerebrally and diplomatically for the sake of his cattle run? Was she, Chris, no more to him than a possibly useful means to an end?

She suddenly realised that she was allowing herself to become too involved—too futilely involved—in Burton Alexander's personal life. It didn't really matter one iota to her how he got hold of Saltbush Flat, or even if he had to marry Jackie Lester to do it . . .

She asked into a tense silence that hung between them, 'Why did you bring me here today, Burton?'

'Why? Because I wanted to make sure you understood the whole set-up here.' He spoke lazily, his eyes narrowed slightly. 'As for the cave, you can count yourself privileged, Christine. I've never before brought anyone to see the Cave of the Winds.'

'Or to be frightened by a goanna?' asked Chris with an attempt at lightness. She didn't feel her question had been answered at all. 'Quite plainly, I'm not at all an outback type.'

'Now just why do you say that? Is it with the idea of getting in first——'

'No,' said Chris. 'You've said it already—quite often. I'm just underlining the obvious.'

He tilted her chin up with a curved finger. 'Do you mean that? Do you mean what I think you mean?'

'How should I know?' Chris stared back at him unblinkingly. 'I just haven't a clue what you think, Burton.'

'None at all.' One arm went around her waist and he began to draw her closer against his body. His finger left her chin and his two hands were clasped behind her back. Chris automatically turned her head aside as he moved to kiss her, but it was to no avail. He was immensely strong, and he was not at all averse to using his strength. Whether she wanted it or not, whether she was compliant or not, she was going to be kissed, and to be kissed relentlessly.

She thought she was going to faint. He held her so closely to him—his lips were forcing her own apart and her whole body seemed on the point of being merged with his . . .

Then he released her so that his arms no longer compelled but simply supported her, and she opened her eyes and looked up at him dazedly, drowningly—wondering what had happened to her, why she had given in so utterly and completely.

'My God, I believe I've kissed you all but into a faint! You're as white as a ghost!'

'You don't know your own strength,' said Chris with a crooked little smile. She thought fleetingly of Francis, much slighter and far less powerful than this man, and she thought of all the kisses they had exchanged. They seemed such innocent, harmless kisses in retrospect, and perhaps Francis had thought of them that way. Perhaps all the intensity, all the seriousness, had been on her side. Very soon now, he and Pam would be actually married. 'And I don't care one little bit,' thought Chris. Why not? Was it because of Burton Alexander? If she lost her heart to him, she'd really be in trouble...

She moved away from Burton, untied the chiffon scarf that held her hair back, and retied it fastidiously and carefully. She asked him casually, 'How was that for the performance of an engaged girl? I thought *you* did very well, Burton. Between us, we'll certainly convince Jackie Lester. But maybe we shouldn't make too good a job of it—she just might not pack it all in and go away. And if you have to play it her way, then *wouldn't* you have a lot of explaining to do?'

A smile that didn't reach his eyes curved his lips. That depression at one end of his mouth hardly showed at all, and his eyes were hard and narrowed.

He said laconically, 'I don't really think so, Christine. But presently I'm going to get you home before I completely forget myself and take you in hand the way I have no right to do. What a pity that ring you're wearing is no more than a pretty showpiece, isn't it?'

'You can have it back as soon as you like,' retorted Christine. 'You've only to say the word——'

'*You're* the one who must say the word, Christine. When you're ready to leave the protection of my home, then you tell me and I'll arrange for you to go. Understand? The ball's continually in your court when it comes to making *that* particular move.' He turned abruptly on his heel and Christine followed him to the jeep beneath a sky which the rapidly westering sun had left an unearthly red. Soon they were weaving a way through a low mulga forest and Chris could smell smoke and honey.

She asked reluctantly, 'We're not going to see those aborigines, are we, Burton?'

'I'm afraid we are,' he said flatly. 'It's against my principles to pass by without greeting my friends. They know well enough that I'm here—they have ways of knowing that.'

'They've heard the jeep——'

'Yes. In addition, they know whose jeep it is, and who's in it. They know that you're here, and that I've taken you to the Cave of the Winds. Maybe they even know the relationship between us— better than we know it ourselves ... Are you coming with me?'

For the life of her, Chris could not say no. And she didn't know whether it was because Burton Alexander wanted her to come or whether she wanted it herself—despite her reluctance.

Now they could see smoke and flames and dark silhouettes through the thin shelter of the trees ahead, and Burton pulled up. Chris climbed from the jeep feeling somehow like a dreamer. There were perhaps twenty or so aborigines around the fire. Some of them wore trousers and shirts, and some, almost naked, had obviously come in from the sandhills. Chris could see the gleam of their eyes and their teeth and she felt nervous and unsure of herself.

They had roasted possums in the fire, then lifted the flesh from the skins and basted it with wild honey, and they were in the midst of a royal feast. She heard a voice call out with relish, 'Dat fella number one tucker, Boss. You and missis like some?'

'No, thank you, Nim,' Burton said with a smile. 'It surely smells good, but I've got to get my white fella missis home before we get lost in the dark.' There was a burst of laughter and he added something else in a language Chris did not understand. After that, the faces all turned her way, and she could feel their eyes on her. She was thankful when goodbyes were said and Burton was taking her back to the jeep.

'It will be pitch-dark before long,' he told her. 'How would you like to spend a night in the bush with me, Christine? Or would you rather we camped here with the natives?'

Chris put her head up.

'You're trying to scare me. You can find your way back to Red Sands, Burton.'

A smile curved his lips and his eyebrows peaked in amusement. 'You believe in me that much, Christine?'

What had Mrs Perry said? 'He'll look after you till his dying day—if you marry him.' Well, she wasn't going to marry him—he hadn't asked her to. But he would look after her, she was certain of it. Even if they had to stay out here with the natives!

She said, 'Yes, I do believe in you, Burton. But please take me home.'

'Right, Christine, I'll take you home.' He looked straight into her eyes, and his amusement had vanished behind a sudden gravity.

Home! Had she said that? She turned away quickly, vaguely troubled. Home. As if home were here—with Burton, on the Red Sands cattle run...

Chris was dead-tired when she got there. So dead-tired that she went straight to bed and didn't know until the morning that Frith Alexander had arrived.

Seen again, and in the light on new knowledge, Frith was disturbingly like that young woman whose face looked out of the photograph in the Red Sands living room. Yet there was an unexpected sturdiness about her that Chris had been unaware of when they met in the city. *Then*, Frith had been an elegant girl in a long evening gown, a swathe of silver-gold hair piled above her narrow face. Here, at Red Sands homestead, in cotton shirt and jeans, her hair sleek against a faintly tanned skin that was innocent of make-up, she had acquired an outdoor character.

Chris thought uneasily and with surprise, 'She belongs—she really belongs.' Yet Burton had implied that she did not belong, that she was too like her mother ever to do so. 'Well,' thought Chris, 'it's not for us to decide her future for her.'

Frith greeted her pleasantly enough over breakfast, in Mrs Perry's presence. Yet Chris imagined a certain constraint. She wondered what Burton had told his sister about his 'engagement', or if the truth was as much a secret from her as from anyone else, and she wondered why she had this vague intimation of hostility. She got through her breakfast feeling ill at ease. She thought Burton might have briefed her as to how she should act in Frith's company instead of going off on the run and leaving her to work things out for herself.

She had gone to tidy her bedroom when Frith knocked on the verandah door and stood lounging there as if she had come to stay. Inwardly, Chris quailed. She hated the situation she had put herself in worse than ever, and had to force herself to go on nonchalantly folding away clothes as if nothing were amiss.

Frith said very deliberately, 'Well, how's the testing time proceeding, Christine? Do you think you might finally decide to settle for the outback, by any chance?'

So that was what Burton had told her, thought Chris making a quick assessment. It was a trial engagement, while Chris made up her mind how she liked the outback. But why should Frith sound so hostile? For hostile she certainly was. It was really coming into the open now, that veiled attitude of the breakfast table.

But what was *she* to say? Being Chris, she could not even pretend not to like it here. She said awkwardly, 'I do like the outback, Frith——'

'You like it—*but*,' said Frith sceptically. 'I think it's a great shame that Burton's caught you on the rebound.'

Chris bit her lip. 'Did Burton tell you *that*?'

'No. I drew my own conclusions. I got myself pretty well mixed up with Richard and your relatives, you know, Christine, and relatives do talk. And I just happen to think that my brother deserves better than that.'

A slow flush had risen to Chris's cheeks. She felt furious with the Gilcrists for talking about her private affairs—about which, she thought, they knew next to nothing. Besides which, they had a poor opinion of her—'a girl with a father like Christine Vance's'. She repeated Frith's words angrily. 'Better than *what*? Better than Christine Vance? Is that what you mean?'

'Good heavens, no!' Frith sounded genuinely shocked. 'Of course I don't mean that. And if Burton wants to marry you—well, now don't get me wrong—that's his affair. I mean what I said before. He's caught you on the rebound.'

A little smile caught suddenly at Chris's mouth and she said, 'You don't want to believe all you hear, Frith.' Instantly, she was surprised at herself. What on earth was she admitting to? About Burton—about Francis——

Frith, quite still in the doorway, watched her keenly from eyes that were almost the blue of Burton's, though they were long and slightly tilted like Amy Alexander's. She asked, after a moment, 'Do you mean you're really in love with my brother?'

There was a slight pause, and then Chris was saved from making a reply by Mrs Perry, who had come into the room with clean towels.

Frith didn't repeat her question when the housekeeper had gone. Instead, she suggested amicably, 'Let's sit out on the verandah, Christine. It's killingly hot already ... You ride, don't you?' she asked a moment later as they sat down, she on the lounger, Chris in a cane chair.

'Yes.'

'Why don't you go out on the run with Burton, then? You can't see much of him or of the place this way, can you, and they both take a lot of knowing.'

Chris looked down at her hands and saw the ruby winking at her guiltily. 'I go out with Burton sometimes. We were out the whole day, yesterday.'

'That was unusual. Mrs Perry told me so when I arrived. And weren't you *dead* when you came in? I can understand *that*—Burton can be quite merciless. I've never enjoyed a day out with him. He has no patience with girls who can't take it.'

'I can't take it,' admitted Chris wryly. 'I certainly was dead when I got in last night.'

Suddenly Frith smiled. She had a wide mouth and fine, straight white teeth, and her smile was reminiscent of Burton's. 'I'm rather putting my foot in it, aren't I? I'm sorry, Christine—it's not that I wouldn't like you for a sister-in-law, but I was feeling a bit on the defensive because—well, Burton's not just anyone.'

'Enough said.' Chris smiled too with relief. She thought Frith was a girl she could be friends with. She didn't pretend, and she would never say one thing and mean another. Again, she was like Burton in that way. It was a great shame there was this inadmissible barrier between them. Chris's reaction to being judged as a girl who had been caught on the rebound was an odd one. She had the most ridiculous feeling of injured innocence, almost as if she were really engaged to Burton. Honesty made her long to tell Frith the truth, but honesty also demanded that she first have Burton's permission.

Which she found she did not get.

Frith was saying moodily, 'I'm always edgy when I come home to Red Sands. The pace is so slow here, after the city, and there's no one about, half the time. I'll tell you what, Chris, why don't we go out to the camp past Five Mile Swamp. They've been mustering for more fats there, and Burton told me last night they'll be branding the cleanskins today.' She added thoughtfully, 'I guess the sale cattle will have to be held at Mittagong Dam now they can't be taken over to Saltbush. It's a frightful mess, by all accounts ... Can you ride a motorbike?'

'I've never tried,' said Chris.

'I must teach you. But not today. You'll have to ride pillion. I'd rather handle a motorbike than a horse any day.

I should have been put on a horse when I was very tiny, but Father seemed to have some phobia that I'd have an accident or something, and I was treated like glass.' She made a face. 'That sort of thing sticks—some of his fear has rubbed off on me ... Change into some jeans, Chris, and grab a hat that will stay on and we'll get moving.'

Chris hurried away, eager to be off. It was certainly going to be different at Red Sands now that Frith was home! She supposed that Burton would be at the muster—unless he was visiting Jackie Lester at Saltbush Flat!

Well, she would soon see.

She spent quite some time after that hanging on to Frith and hoping she would not be bumped off as they rattled over the rough ground, through mulga and spinifex, following a set of clearly marked wheel tracks. In a cloud of red dust, away to the east across the plain, they caught sight of a slowly moving mob of cattle. Frith slowed down enough for Chris to hear her shout over her shoulder, 'Those will be cattle for the sale—heading for Mittagong Dam. I'd like to know how Burton plans to fatten *them* up, now Saltbush has gone down the drain.'

It was not long after that they reached the branding camp, a scene of hectic activity. Frith braked carelessly under a tree, and stuck one dusty foot negligently on the ground, and for a moment they both sat silently surveying the scene. In the shelter of a long low range was a great mob of cattle, and branding was in progress. Every so often in the general mêlée, a beast was released and went lumbering off into the shelter of the mulga. It took Chris, standing in the shade now, some time to accustom her eyes to the dust and the glare and the haze, or to make much sense of the scene at all. But Frith stared avidly, biting nervously on her lower lip, her fingers stuck in her narrow belt in a stance that reminded Chris acutely of Burton. She might take after her mother to a large degree, but Chris reflected that there must be something of their father in both of them, for they were alike in several odd ways. Frith's black stetson had fallen back and hung around her neck by its strap, and the sun, slanting through the trees, struck a metallic glitter off her brilliant hair. There was a strange look of excitement on her face, and it made Chris wonder about her—the girl who must live out her life in the city because her father had decided it that way. The girl whose mother, at twenty-one, had walked out into the burning beckoning heat of the red sandhills and disappeared for ever.

Chris pulled the brim of her hat down over her eyes and looked over at the camp again. In all that dust and confusion she could not possibly tell if Burton was there, giving orders and seeing that everything went as it should. There was a smell of singed hair and scorched flesh, and the dust was rising red and thick. Chris had glimpses of rolling eyes and rippling muscles as a huge beast struggled to its feet and staggered off. It was all muscle and power and panic— a man's world entirely. Chris felt slightly sickened, but she was fascinated nonetheless, and soon her attention was riveted on a tall broad-shouldered stockman whose cord trousers and dark shirt were streaked with dust. He wore a black and red scarf knotted at his throat, his hat was pulled well down over his eyes, and his power and forcefulness, his economy of movement and effort, were magnificent to watch.

Her eyes followed him time after time as he seized an animal, be it calf or full-grown weighty beast, by the neck and threw it easily to the ground. Then, while his offsider knelt on the animal's neck, he clipped its ear and branded it with such swiftness and sureness that she was utterly fascinated and could not keep her eyes off him. The smell of burning hair was in her nostrils, waves of dust floated by on hot winds, the branding irons glowed red and smoke mingled with the dust.

It was a seething, tumultuous scene, and for Chris that one stockman stood out among a collection of dust-hazed silhouettes—a figure etched in fire.

She was not quite certain when it was that she realised who the stockman in the dark neckerchief was, and then a shock went through her like a lightning flash. For it was, of course, Burton Alexander.

Chris glanced quickly, almost guiltily, at Frith to see if she too were watching his movements. But Frith's eyes were on the fringe of the mob, following a rider there who was bringing back a recalcitrant hunk of beef. Her interest, Chris decided—quite wrongly, as it happened—was a sheerly impersonal one.

Almost without her volition, her attention returned to Burton. Somehow, she had never pictured him doing quite this sort of work—burning the Red Sands brand into the hide of his cattle. She had not known that his personality could become so completely submerged that he could equate himself in every way with his own stockmen. Yet that was how it was in the outback. If a man was to win, he must be able to work—to do a man's work in a man's world. Suddenly she saw him as immensely distant from her own world—immensely unattainable.

'And yet he bothers with me,' she thought soberly. 'He has an irritated sort of patience with my—indecisions.'

She had reached this point in her reflections when she discovered that he had at last escaped her vision. She searched for him in the red swirling dust, but he was no-where to be seen. Frith—Frith was still intent on her horse-man, and Chris was straining her eyes again in a futile search for Burton when a rider on a black horse came tear-ing out of the dust, full tilt towards the trees where she and Frith were standing.

She felt her legs ready to give way beneath her. Her heart had suddenly begun to beat madly as it had when the iguana raced towards her. It was a ridiculous thought, but she could not even smile at it. She watched the rider on the black horse come hell for leather towards her. She saw the black and red scarf at his throat as with a flurry of dust and a sudden swerve the horse stopped stock-still a yard away.

Burton leaned down with a greeting.

'What are you two girls doing out here?'

Well, it was a greeting of sorts!

Frith said calmly, 'I brought Chris out to see what goes on.'

'Did you now!' He looked down at Frith, then at Christine, and then over his shoulder where the cattle were.

Frith said in an odd almost defiant tone, her voice wavering faintly, 'I see Paddy's still performing wonders for you.'

'He's doing a good job, which is no more than I expect of him,' Burton said curtly.

'I might go over and say hello,' said Frith, and Chris's ears pricked up. Mrs Perry had said—oh, such an age ago! —that Paddy was a favourite with Frith—and that Burton didn't like it. So she was not surprised when he said, 'There's no need for that.'

'Just for old times' sake,' said Frith airily. 'And because Paddy won't come and say hello to me—and he really should, you know, seeing I'm the Boss's sister.'

'He probably doesn't even know you're here,' said Burton.

'Then I'll let him know.' With a quick movement, she was on the motorbike and with a roar had taken off to the other side of the cattle, giving it a wide berth. There, Chris saw the stockman she had been watching so avidly. He was lighting a cigarette and walking his horse. So that was Paddy Preston! He, like all the others, was apparently knocking off for lunch.

Burton's eyes followed his sister worriedly for a minute, then he gave his attention to Christine.

'Are you two girls getting on together, Christine?'

'Yes,' said Chris briefly. 'What did you tell her—about us?'

'Haven't you found that out? Didn't you get in first with a full confession?'

'No, but I'd like to—with your permission.'

'Well, you're not going to have that. It's something between you and me only, and don't you forget it.'

'I haven't,' said Chris resentfully.

He flashed her a sudden hard smile. 'I respect you for that.'

'Well, that's something,' said Chris.

'What?'

'To have your respect.'

He looked at her hard, and she looked back at him, noticing how streaked with dust and perspiration his face was. He looked a stranger—a rough, tough stockman. And yet his eyes were the soft, hyacinth-blue eyes that she knew so well. He asked quizzically, 'Do you want more than respect from me, then, Chris?'

She knew suddenly that she did. She wanted a great deal more than his respect. Yet to have his respect was important too, and she was aware of it. She said, keeping her voice and her gaze steady, 'No, thank you. Your respect will do very nicely, Burton.' Her gaze went past the black horse, to where she could see Frith talking to Paddy, and she asked rather wildly, inconsequentially, 'Who's Paddy?'

'My overseer—Paddy Preston. Surely you know that.'

'Surely? *You* haven't told me much.'

'No. But you might have asked someone else—during your convalescence. Or,' he added, screwing his eyes up, 'Frith could have told you.'

'Neither of us has indulged in girlish confidences.'

'Then keep it that way,' he said tersely. He swung his horse's head and moved away from her, leaving her to stand alone beneath the trees. He rode over to Frith, who in a moment came back on her motorcycle, her colour high.

'Let's get out of here. I simply couldn't bear to partake of hunks of steak and damper.' She waited for Chris to take the pillion seat, and in another moment they roared off across the plain in a cloud of dust. 'I sometimes wonder why I ever come back to Red Sands,' she shouted back over her shoulder. 'Once those men get out to the camp, they're insufferable. Paddy Preston can hardly bother to be civil to me, yet I've known him since I was a schoolgirl. As for Burton—what a welcome! It seems it's something of a crime to be a female, on this run.'

There was a touch of hysteria in her voice, and Chris wondered silently who had upset her most, Burton or the overseer. She rather thought it was the latter...

By evening, Frith had calmed down again. Both girls had taken a siesta, and later, Frith had gone to the waterhole for a swim. Chris wished she had been invited along, but after all, she was not Frith's guest. By the time Burton returned from the muster, had showered and come to the sitting room, Frith was completely calm and self-possessed, and looked very much the city girl in a fine cotton dress with an abstract pattern of white, silver-grey and tangerine. Burton poured the drinks, and Frith said, 'Play something sentimental on the piano, Burton. It soothes the savage breast, besides which, it's a sure way to any girl's heart.' She sent Chris the vestige of a smile.

'Surely the savage breast's have been soothed already,' said Burton carelessly. 'Maybe after dinner. I'm not in the mood for winning heart's right now. I'm tired, and I'm hungry. What do you say, Chris? Can you wait an hour or two for me to woo you?'

His look, slanting, and slightly mocking made Chris colour, and she hoped Frith would not notice. Something very odd was happening in the region of her heart. There was something about the expression in Burton's eyes ... Of course, he was putting on a show for Frith's benefit, but she wished that he wouldn't. She managed to say with only a slight tremor, 'Yes, I can wait.'

When later she left her chair to go in to dinner, he put an arm around her waist, and, as they moved across the room, stooped to kiss her lightly on the lips.

'We haven't exchanged a single kiss today, have we?' His eyes looked into hers and there was a little malice in them. 'Hardly fair of me when you came all that way on a motorbike to see me this morning. You're becoming quite the little country girl after all, aren't you? Was it enlightening?'

'Most,' said Chris, trying to speak as banteringly as he was. It had been enlightening—she had discovered something about herself and her feelings for Burton that she had not yet dared to look back at. It was like a dream. If one recalled it immediately on awakening, one recalled it in all its clarity, but if one got on with the business of living, one remembered only fleetingly. So it was with what had happened to her today. She could not quite call back the emotion she had experienced when she had discovered it was Burton Alexander she had been watching so intently, or when he had come thundering out of the dust towards her ...

After dinner, Mrs Perry went to listen to her wireless while the other three sat out on the verandah. Burton refused to play the piano.

'I want to hear what you have to say for yourself, Frith. What's brought you rushing headlong to Red Sands, and what's happened to that excellent job you've been holding down? I don't want you to become a rolling stone.'

'But I *am* a rolling stone,' said Frith. 'And you might as well know—I've tossed in my job.'

'Why? You liked it, and you were doing well—very well.'

Frith sighed and moved restlessly. Chris had a more than vague suspicion that Paddy Preston could be the reason for Frith's return to the outback. She wondered if she should make herself scarce. It was hardly her business to listen in on a family session like this. But before she could make more than the slightest move, Burton's hand had closed around her wrist, and he said irritably, 'For goodness' sake, don't imagine you have to go tiptoeing off, Chris. You're part of the family and you might as well hear our secrets.'

'Frith may think differently.' She was intensely aware that he had started to call her Chris instead of Christine, and wondered why—or if there were any reason at all. 'Besides, I'm not part of the family.'

Frith said brightly, 'Stay where you are, Christine. I've got nothing to hide. Burton always has a go at me when I come home. For some reason or other he thinks I should be perfectly happy in the city. As for my job, it was a very mediocre one. I can't imagine why Father and Burton have always been so sure I was destined to perform wonders of some kind in the big world——'

'You're exaggerating, my girl,' said Burton irritably. He reached for cigarettes, and only then released Chris's wrist, which felt as if it were encircled by a flame. She could smell the yellow jasmine, and her eyes burned with the image of Burton's face as he had looked down at her this morning—a face dusty and sweat-stained and hard, the blue eyes looking at her so intently. 'If you would only realise it,' he was telling Frith as he struck a match and held it steady before lighting his cigarette, 'you're very fortunate to have menfolk who recognise your artistic talent and want you to have the opportunity to develop it.'

'I wouldn't say you'd *recognised* it,' said Frith. 'I'd say you'd pushed it—both you and Father. It's a bit of a joke really, Christine. I only got into art school by the skin of my teeth—I remember that, Burton, even if you don't. And now about all I can achieve is a gimmicky kind of fashion drawing that's not going to stay popular much longer, and *then* what's to become of me? I've been bluffing my way along with these kinky figures with legs about three yards long and weird little heads that wouldn't hold more than an eggspoon of brains!'

'You underrate yourself, Frith,' said Burton irritably. 'That's a lot of rubbish—you have a very clever fashion style.'

'Clever!' scoffed Frith. 'Honestly, Burton, I often think life would have been a lot easier for me if I hadn't been given such a crazy name.' She turned to Chris with a wry grimace. '*Frith!* Could anything be weirder? And of course I'm expected to do something spectacular to justify it. Actually, my name's Amy, after my mother. Amy Frith Alexander. I just wish I could be called Amy and settle down happily in the bush. But Father couldn't bear to call me Amy, on account of my mother dying so young, when I was a tiny baby.'

Burton said caustically, 'No matter what you were called,

my girl, you'd never settle down happily out here. You haven't the temperament. You don't even like horses ... But all this is beside the point—an excuse for giving up your job and rushing back here. What's happened between you and Richard Gilcrist?'

'I thought that was coming,' said Frith. 'And I'm sorry to disappoint you, but nothing's happened. Richard's gone back to the M.I.A., that's all. Please just don't try to push me into matrimony, Burton. You stay out of my love life and I'll stay out of yours.'

Burton was silent and Chris had the feeling he was angry. Then as if in tune with his mood, a sudden flash of lightning lit up the sky far, far away, low on the horizon. It was followed by another and another, and thunder growled distantly. In those lightning flashes, Chris saw the first clouds she had seen since coming to Red Sands.

'If only it would rain!' Frith exclaimed as they all watched the display. 'That would save the day, Burton. You'd have feed enough to fatten up that stock of yours, and Jackie Lester could do what she liked with Saltbush Flat.'

'Don't you believe it,' said Burton laconically. 'We shan't ever have enough rain for that. And right now, maybe a bit of water will run into the creeks from higher up, but there'll be no feed sprouting overnight. And even if by some miracle we were saved this season, I still need Saltbush Flat, and I'm going to have it—and that pretty soon.' He heaved himself out of his chair and held out a hand to Christine. 'Come and take a walk in the garden, Chris. There's no air around the house. And Frith'—he pulled Chris to her feet as he spoke and put an arm casually around her waist—'I'd think a bit further about young Gilcrist if I were you. I'm not trying to push you, only to make you a bit more serious-minded.'

Frith's silence had a quality of obstinacy in it, and she did not respond to his smile.

Once they were away from the house and walking among the orange trees, Chris moved away from Burton. 'You don't have to hang on to me any longer. May I go inside now?'

'No, you may not. I brought you out here with a specific object in mind.'

'To kiss me in full view of the verandah?'

'No. To warn you that Frith doesn't know how her mother lost her life—and to ensure that I can have confidence in your discretion.'

It took Chris a moment to absorb what he had said. First and foremost in her mind was an illogical sense of having been rebuffed. Her mind had leaped when he had suggested a walk in the garden. Instinctively, she had anticipated being kissed. And she had wanted it to happen—to prove or to disprove something to herself. Instead, Burton had demonstrated something else to her—that he was not interested in kissing her. She said acidly, from her sense of hurt, 'I think the whole set-up's idiotic. Why shouldn't Frith know the truth? She's adult.'

'She's also extremely sensitive and impressionable.'

'You mean she could become—unbalanced, like her mother? I think that's nonsense.' He had begun to walk more briskly and she hurried along in his wake, aware of a strong desire to argue with him, however senselessly—to go against him, to assert herself. 'You're not a psychologist. You're a cattle man.'

He ignored that. 'Frith has her mother's temperament.'

'How do you know? You were only a boy when——'

'I know what my father told me,' he said harshly. 'And I know how I felt when I was eighteen and heard the truth about Amy. I remember my nightmares—my horror of that house that was already beginning to crumble away, of those long red relentless sandhills, so hungry and beckoning. They seemed almost to beckon to me ... So shut up, and allow me to decide what's best for my sister. Will you do that? Because if not——'

'If not, then I had better go? That would suit me,' flared Chris, inwardly ashamed of herself and hardly aware of what she was saying. 'There's nothing I'd like better. If you think it's fun being pushed around here, just so you can get Saltbush Flat the painless way—What's more, being handed out treacly kisses to prove we're engaged, and taken for a walk in the garden so Frith will think you're feeling romantic. And in spite of all the fuss, I know what will happen eventually—you'll marry Jackie Lester for economic reasons. Oh, I hate the whole stupid situation!'

Her angry voice stopped suddenly as he turned on her, took her by the shoulders and swung her forcibly against his body, pressing his lips to hers in a kiss that had no tenderness in it, but bruised and hurt. Chris could feel his heart pounding as hard as her own. *Her* heart's hurry was from anger, but she didn't know why his heart should be so hard at work...

'There!' he said at last. 'That will teach you to be so bad-tempered, Christine. The trouble with you is that you're frustrated—like a little old maid. You need a bit of honest loving up. Come back into my arms and I'll soothe you some more, and we'll see if you change your tune.'

'No!' said Chris, more furious than ever. 'Leave me alone.' She knew that she wanted more than anything to be pulled back into his arms—but not if it was simply because he thought she was suffering from frustration. She didn't want to be handed out kisses as a sort of medicine...

'Why? Are you remembering Francis Rogeon's kisses—telling yourself that no man can kiss as he did? I promise you I could soon make you forget all about that! I guarantee I've had more experience than your young vigneron.'

'I'm quite willing to believe you,' retorted Chris. Her lips were burning, her whole body was burning, and now to add to the turmoil in her mind, brilliant lightning shot across the dark sky, followed by a thunder roll that made her put her hands to her ears.

'You see?' said Burton, with a trace of amusement. 'The elements are co-operating with me in chastening you. Which reminds me of what I was about to say when you decided so hastily that I was going to tell you you could leave my homestead. It was simply this. If you're determined to air your limited views about what's good for my sister and what's not, then I shall here and now put you over my knee and give you a sound spanking.'

'No, you will not,' said Chris, outraged. 'I'm not so spineless that I would put up with *that*.'

'Not spineless,' he agreed, 'but physically weaker than I am. By the time you'd shouted and someone had come, it would be all over.'

Chris eyed him. and rememembered how he had handled the cattle that morning—only that morning, yet it seemed an age ago!—and she realised anew how little she really knew about him. He was so much older and more worldly than Francis had been. She was suddenly uncertain, almost defeated. Another flash of lightning made her close her eyes and clench her teeth, and suddenly Burton laughed and put his arm around her shoulder.

'Let's get back to the homestead. And be comforted, my Christine—the moment when I experienced that almost irresistible urge to spank you is long past. Besides, I have more than a little respect for your ego. Believe it or not, I really do have a rough and rudimentary understanding of the working of the feminine mind.'

'Not of my mind,' said Chris, trying to decide whether or not to let his arm stay where it was, and meanwhile doing nothing about it.

He laughed again. 'You're an exceedingly contra-suggestible young woman.' He said it so good-humouredly, so tolerantly, that Chris felt ashamed of her rather childish outburst. It was good to walk beside him like this, his arm about her, and she said with an effort, 'Of course I shan't betray your confidence—about Frith's mother. And I *am* contra-suggestible. It's a habit, I'm afraid, acquired from having all those Gilcrists push me around.'

'Never mind. You haven't been too bad while you've been under my protection. And after all, one expects a bit of temperament with hair like yours.'

He was smiling at her as they stepped up into the verandah again, and Chris thought with faint regret that they must have presented a picture of two happy lovers to Frith, who still sat there.

It was only later on, alone in her room, that she realised he had not contradicted her suggestion that he would eventually marry Jackie Lester...

CHAPTER SIX

STRANGELY enough, after their little brush, Burton seemed to set himself out to be agreeable and friendly, and during the next few days he took time off now and again to join Christine and Frith at the waterhole, and once, stayed on there for an evening picnic. Chris found it hard to believe it could be solely on her account, and wondered if it was mainly on Frith's. None of the three motorbikes that belonged to the station appeared to be available—they were all being used by the stockmen—and Chris suspected that Burton was trying to make sure that his sister kept away from the overseer, Paddy Preston.

The creeks were running now, although there had been no rain around the homestead. And when, some nights later, there were more thunderstorms out on the horizon, Burton said that he would fly out to see how his run had fared, and promised to take both the girls with him.

The following morning when Chris came out to breakfast somewhat earlier than usual, Burton had already gone out on the run, and it appeared that Frith had gone too. Her disappointment was hard to bear, and made her realise more clearly than anything else had done just how much she was attracted to Burton. It was more than that, of course. She was in love with him. But it would never do, and the very recognition of the fact was enough to send her into a mild panic. Love, in her limited experience, was apt to deal out some hard blows. She didn't want ever again to go through what she had suffered when Francis had dropped her. So if Burton and Frith had gone out together—if they neglected to come in and fetch her before they took the plane up—then she must simply snap her fingers and forget the whole thing. Forget the Alexander family in its entirety, carry on coldbloodedly with the pretence of being Burton's fiancée, and start some really serious thinking about what she was going to do with herself the minute— the very minute!—he had ceased to need her 'co-operation.' That minute would come possibly when Jackie Lester grew fed up with Saltbush Flat and with trying to use it as bait to catch the boss of Red Sands; or, alternatively, when Burton found he could hold out no longer— when it became imperative that he should get possession of those pastures on Saltbush to fatten his cattle for market. Then he would have to give in, Chris was certain, however much it went against the grain. *Then*, it would be economic to accept Jackie's unspoken terms.

Chris, eating her breakfast alone on the verandah, glanced out across the garden at the cloudless blue sky, wondering hopefully if it might possibly have rained up in the north-eastern corner of the run, around Copper Burr Bore, and if that rain would have been enough to make the grass spring up richly so that the cattle could be fattened there, thereby granting Burton a reprieve.

Burton? Chris wondered wryly. Or Christine Vance?

She left her coffee to cool and sauntered along the verandah to the place where they had sat last night, watching the storm. There was a gap in the trees that grew around the house there, and one could see right out across the plain. She stood by the rail staring out intently. Did it look misty on the horizon—vaguely grey? Chris was sure it did. It was not heat haze dancing. It must be rain—it *must* be ...

She started when Frith suddenly appeared on the path in jeans and shirt and riding boots. Frith in riding boots! Chris's surprise at this was uppermost after her first instant feeling of relief that the Alexanders had not, after all, gone away without her. Her spirits soared and she smiled cheerfully at Frith and asked, 'Am I wrong, or have you been riding?'

Frith gave a wry smile. 'You're not wrong. I've been riding—if you can call it that. And I've a feeling I'm going to be sore and sorry.' She came up the verandah steps stiffly. 'I thought it was about time I stopped being so docile. It's pretty feeble to keep blaming the fact that you can't ride and don't like horses on your family, isn't it?' She leaned tenderly against the rail. 'So I got to thinking, and as soon as Burton had gone, I got Joe to saddle up White Star for me. She's the most tractable little creature you can imagine, let's not pretend, and off I went. Not what you'd call really pleasurable, but I didn't do too badly. Actually, I got well on the way to Long Bore. It's a track White Star knows, and I happened to run into Paddy Preston.' There was a sparkle in her blue eyes, and her tanned cheeks were faintly coloured. 'Now I'm ravenous— ready for more breakfast!'

'Will you tell Burton?' Chris asked as they went back along the verandah together.

'What? That I saw Paddy?' Frith's colour deepened and she corrected herself hastily, 'Oh, you mean that I went out riding. No, that can wait until I've improved my style a bit.'

'And Paddy won't mention it.'

Frith shrugged and disappeared in the direction of the kitchen, to appear a couple of minutes later with a large grapefruit and a jug of coffee.

Chris found she could no longer contain her curiosity and decided to fish. After all, she argued with herself, Frith knows all sorts of things about me. Why shouldn't I know something about her? She asked, sounding only mildly interested, 'Paddy Preston's the overseer here, isn't he? Do you know, I've never met him?'

'Been warned to steer clear of him?' Frith did not raise her eyes as she sprinkled sugar on her grapefruit and prepared to eat it.

'No. Should I have been?'

'I don't really know. Sometimes I get the idea that Burton thinks Paddy's not a nice man to know—even though they were at school together.'

'If he thinks that, would he have him working here?'

'Maybe he would. It's good for Red Sands. Burton depends a lot on Paddy. His whole life is handling cattle—I guess he even dreams it. And can he handle them! Did you notice him the other day when we went out on the bike?'

'I believe I did. But Burton's just as good, isn't he?'

Frith laughed. 'Well, *you*'d think so. But yes—Burton can do what he likes with cattle. But you see, he's the boss. Paddy spends most of his life out on the run getting the cattle used to handling. You can't expect that of the boss—not on a run this size. The homestead's *his* headquarters. But the cattle must be well behaved when the buyers come in to look them over, you see—that cuts a lot of ice. Well-handled cattle bring in a far better price than a wild, undisciplined lot. Burton could never let Paddy go.'

There was an odd timbre in her voice and a hunger in her eyes, and Chris wondered not for the first time if Paddy Preston was the reason Frith was not interested in Richard Gilcrist. Yet Burton had insisted that Frith was not an outback girl. Chris didn't know if he was wrong or right...

Later, Burton came back, picked up the jeep and took the girls out to the station airstrip, and they went up in his small aircraft to see exactly what was happening around the Copper Burr Bore. The creeks there were certainly running. Chris could see brown frothing torrents racing across the red plain and yet the earth looked as dry and hungry as ever.

Frith was openly disappointed. 'It must have been further out. How rotten! I was hoping you'd be able to tell Jackie Lester to go to hell——'

'I hardly think I should do that in any case,' said Burton grimly. 'Feed here wouldn't solve even my most immediate problem. By the time I got my cattle all this way they'd have lost more condition than they could pick up again in the limited time at our disposal. No, I've got to have Saltbush, that's for sure.'

Chris's spirits sagged. Without knowing it, she had been more or less counting on a miracle. The thought of Burton marrying Jackie Lester was abhorrent to her, but she did not doubt that he would do it. After all, Francis Rogeon had done more or less the same thing when he opted for Pam. He needed money for more vines, for up-to-date equipment. Burton had position, money, everything except one little corner of the world that was essential to him. So of course he would marry Jackie Lester to get it. *Her* mistake was in falling in love with him.

'Okay,' she thought, 'let's get it over.' She wished that he would take his plane down here and now, see Jackie and get it all settled. Then she would leave Red Sands, and somehow or other she would get through the next few years of her life. How, she did not know. Right now, her future looked just a great big blank.

Frith said, 'Let's go over Saltbush, Burton,' and Burton obligingly turned the plane and flew south, and in no time at all they were looking down on the green pastures that Chris had seen before.

Frith said bitterly, 'And not a single solitary beast there to enjoy it all and grow a nice shiny coat. It's criminal! I just can't think why Arthur Lester ever left the place to that girl—especially as he hadn't seen her since she was practically an infant. It would have been my bet that he'd have left it to you, Burton. In fact, I'm sure I heard him say once that he would.'

'It's been common knowledge for years who was to have Saltbush,' said Burton laconically. 'Arthur told us long, long ago when he made a will in Jackie's favour. You'd have been too young to take any notice then, Frith.'

'But *since* then,' Frith insisted. Her blue eyes were thoughtful. 'I'd really like to give that girl a piece of my mind.'

'You'll leave her alone.' Burton spoke sharply. 'It's not

her fault she was left a place that's a bone of contention. She'll be off back to the city in her own good time. It's lonely at Saltbush.'

Now they were flying directly over the small homestead, and Frith said, 'Well, she's not gone yet. I can see her down there looking like a pretty little pink daisy. What *is* she like?'

'Ask Chris,' said her brother carelessly. 'She's been to visit.' He banked and turned and the plane gained altitude, and Frith said insistently, 'Well, let's have it, Chris—what's your opinion of the girl at Saltbush Flat?'

Chris thought Burton could have given a better description than she could—he saw her every day! She said lamely, 'She's—well, she *is* a little like a pretty pink daisy. But she's practical too. She's been growing seedlings and painting out the house, and making soft furnishings——'

'Good heavens! She's really digging herself in. I wonder why?' mused Frith innocently.

Burton cast Chris a cynically amused glance. 'You must think about it, Frith. One of these days you might come up with the answer. And by the way, Chris, Jackie hasn't progressed very far with the home decorating. I don't think she's really such a great hand at it.'

By now they were almost back at the Red Sands airstrip, the plane was losing altitude, and Chris was thoughtful. Why wasn't Jackie progressing with her home-making? Was it a case of too much company—Burton's company? Or was she certain now that she would be moving over to Red Sands, so long as she held her ground? Despite the fact that she looked like a pretty doll, the girl was surely no fool . . .

A few minutes later, while Burton helped Chris down into the sizzling sunlight on the airstrip, Frith wandered ahead to the jeep. Burton held Chris back for a moment, his arm about her waist, so that a sudden tremor went through her. He smiled down into her eyes, and because she had not drawn away from him, told her, 'Your act is improving, Chris. We're beginning to make quite a team, aren't we?'

She managed a smile. 'We're getting used to each other. But it's a bit of a waste, isn't it, seeing Jackie Lester can't see us.'

'The time will come,' he assured her off-handedly. 'You haven't hinted to Frith that ours is not a regular arrangement?' He cocked an eyebrow, looking down from his rugged height. His blond-streaked hair was tousled, and his shirt was undone to the waist, against the heat, and he spoke in a low intimate voice that did odd things to Chris's heart. It was worse than listening to him playing that Chopin nocturne last night, she thought. She had almost died with with the pleasure of that. It had been the most utterly sensual thing she had ever heard against the deep silence of the outback night.

Now she answered his question shakily. 'Of course not.'

'I must admit you're a very pleasant surprise, Chris. Both lovely to look at and discreet. I'm grateful I can trust you, and while I know it's hard on you, I'd rather not confide in Frith. It's wisest not to extend the number of those in the know.'

'Flattery,' thought Chris bleakly, because it had been sweet to hear him call her lovely to look at. 'Flattery to gain my allegiance.'

Frith, who had reached the jeep, called, 'Come on, you two. Can't all that stuff wait till tonight? I'm parched.'

When they were driving back to the homestead, she took up the previous subject once more.

'I think it's unjust about Saltbush. You were Arthur's best friend, Burton. Oh, I know he had all those mates of his in the town, who were always happy to have him shout them a drink. But the way he threw his money around putting down bores as though he were going to strike a goldmine or something, he'd have been bankrupt without your help.'

Burton shrugged. 'It was to my own advantage to finance some of those bores. It kept Arthur happy and the water is useful. I can't complain.'

'And now this dopey girl's got the lot. Has she got money

of her own as well, Burton?'

'Not a cracker, as far as I know. Poor child, she lost her father when she was a tot.' He braked as they reached the gravel yard.

'Then what's she living on, over there? And who's paying for her home-decorating outfit?'

'That's the sixty-four-dollar question,' said Burton with a grin. 'Excuse me— I'll leave you girls to have lunch. I want to get back to the muster.'

He strode off and Frith said, '*He*'s financing it all, of course. I can't think why. Sometimes I think he *likes* that girl at Saltbush Flat.' She looked at Chris as the two girls walked through the garden. 'Does it worry you at all, Christine?'

'What?' asked Chris blankly.

'That there's another girl around and that she's being practically supported by your fiancé.'

Chris coloured deeply and turned her head away.

'Not really.'

'It would me, if I were really keen. *Are* you really keen, Chris?'

'On Burton?' They had reached the shade of the verandah, and Chris paused at the door of her bedroom, her back half turned.

'On Burton—and on Red Sands.'

'What do you think?' Chris said enigmatically. She looked back and managed a smile. Her cheeks were flushed and her heart hammering. 'See you at lunch.'

When she went into her room, the first thing she saw was the calendar that hung on the wall, a certain date outlined with a heavy black line. Francis's wedding date. 'Do I care at all?' she asked herself. She looked at herself in the dressing table mirror. Clear grey eyes looked back at her, her hair hung over one shoulder in a red, defiant twist. She looked very much alive and well! 'No,' she told her reflection, 'I don't care one little bit. It's all over.' She licked her lips with a pink tongue and made a face at herself. She hoped she was not getting herself into a worse mess than ever. Better make plans for the future! But she knew she would not—and she did not. She simply stayed on at Red Sands.

Frith went out riding alone often after that day. She never asked Chris to join her, which was disappointing, for Chris liked Burton's sister.

More out of kindness than for any other reason, Chris called in to see Peg Spencer now and again. She hadn't much sympathy with her and they had little in common, and Chris grew tired of listening to eternal complaints about the heat, and boredom, and the lack of understanding from the menfolk. Chris knew that Burton understood Peg's situation very well indeed—and that it gave him no satisfaction to have his book-keeper's wife unhappy and discontented. He had told Chris that Dan was to leave. Peg was her husband's problem—'He married her, God knows why,' Burton had said wearily. 'She has no brains and no character and only a modicum of beauty'...

One day Frith came home well into the afternoon and joined Chris who was sitting on the verandah after her siesta.

'I took White Star and went to see that girl at Saltbush Flat.' She flung herself into a chair, her blue eyes stormy, her legs stretched out in front of her, and tipped back her silvery blonde head. 'She's having a wonderful time over there. Burton talks so glibly of how lonely she's going to find it and all the while he's dashing in to see that she's all right. He and Paddy and heaven knows who else. I tell you, Chris, it's pretty quiet here in comparison to the way it is at Saltbush Flat!' She looked up suddenly. 'You'd better watch out. That girl means to find herself a husband out here. If she can't have Burton, then she's going to have Paddy. Either way, she holds an ace.'

Chris, though her heart was thudding, said calmly, 'Saltbush Flat? Well, I knew that.'

'You knew it? Then don't you care? Is it true what she says, that you're not really in love with Burton? Do you know that he goes over there——'

120

'Yes, I know. He takes her fresh supplies——'

'But every day! And they're on kissing terms—or so she says.'

Chris tried not to think of that. 'And—Paddy Preston?'

Frith's delicate nostrils flared slightly. 'Paddy I saw for myself. He was very busy making a proper job of kissing her. Paddy wouldn't say no to Saltbush Flat ... I just can't understand my brother. Why doesn't he pay the girl whatever she wants and get rid of her?'

She glared almost accusingly at Chris, who said mildly, 'You'll have to ask Burton that yourself, Frith. It's no use looking at me.'

'If you were someone else,' said Frith, jumping up angrily, 'instead of a girl who's made a fool of herself over some man, you wouldn't sit twiddling your thumbs. You'd use your influence. You'd insist Burton get rid of her, but fast! Don't you *care* about Burton or Red Sands or anything at all?'

Chris stared at her speechlessly. Of course she cared about Burton and Red Sands, but she could not use her influence, and it was not for the reason that Frith suggested —though a raw place was touched by that gibe. A girl who's made a fool of herself—that was the way the Gilcrists saw her. She said at last with a slow emphasis, 'I can't dictate to Burton what he should do. And anyhow, if Paddy Preston marries Jackie, then won't he lease those pastures to Burton?'

'Oh!' Frith all but stamped her foot, and there were actually tears in her eyes. 'I had no idea you were so *unfeeling*!' She turned on her heel and fled.

Chris went rather thoughtfully to her room to change for dinner. She was sure Frith was in love with Paddy Preston. And she was sure too that Jackie was going to win her battle. She was little, but she was determined. Chris didn't think Paddy Preston really came into the picture at all—Jackie was after bigger fish than the overseer. It was Burton —that 'gorgeous hunk of a man'—with whom she had fallen in love. In her shallow way, thought Chris.

She had changed into a fresh dress and was staring absently but bleakly at her wall calendar, wondering how long it would be before she would have to go, when she became aware of a shadow in the doorway. She turned her head and Burton stood there. He had just come in from the run. His shirt was crumpled and a lock of hair fell across his forehead. His blue eyes blazed scornfully from a face that was dust-stained and weary, and his teeth showed white as he said almost savagely, 'Are you still whipping a dead horse, Christine? Isn't it time you grew up and stopped hanging on the tail of a schoolgirl love affair?'

Chris felt jolted. 'Do you want me to hurry up and leave your—*protection*—so that you can settle your affair with Jackie Lester?'

'What do you mean by that?' His hands were on his hips and fury glinted plainly in his eyes.

'I'm not a complete fool,' said Chris. 'I know how urgent the situation's becoming here. You can't want me on your conscience much longer. Well, don't worry, you can take your ring back and I'll get out of your hair just as soon as you like. Gladly.'

'We've been over that before,' he rapped. 'I don't want my ring back.'

'I'm going to give it back just the same,' said Chris. To her amazement, he suddenly stepped forward and snatched the calendar off the wall and flung it on the floor.

'That will be one less thing to keep your memories alive. Moping over that day after day! Wake up, Christine, and take a look at the present—at what's going on right under your eyes.' He had her by the wrist and drew her against him with one fierce sweeping gesture. 'Come on now—look at me, for a start. Tell me what you see.'

Chris, whose eyes were riveted on his, had begun to shake. His face was so close to hers now that she could see every particle of dust on his cheeks, every fine pale line that showed around his eyes. She could see the lines that radiated from his pupils, deep violet blue against a lighter blue background, and she thought vaguely, 'That's why they

122

look like hyacinths.' She could see the dust on his thick eyelashes, and she could feel it on his hands as they gripped her. It was in her nostrils—it was everywhere—the red dust of the desert country.

She said huskily, 'I see dust, Burton. You've been riding in the dust all day.'

His pupils darkened and she saw shock in his eyes. His hold on her grew fiercer. 'So that's what you see,' he bit out. 'I'm filthy, aren't I? Would you like to be married to me, Christine?—married to a man who lives a cattleman's life? Who comes home covered in dust and sweat every evening, and can't wait to take you in his arms—just the way I'm taking you now. Who can't wait to have his lips against yours or to feel your heart pounding against his own. *Is* your heart pounding, Christine?' One hand was suddenly on her breast, and she knew that her heart was pounding very hard and that it was intolerable that he should discover it...

Somehow, she flung away from him, biting hard on her lip, her lashes hiding her eyes because she could not bear either that he should read what they were saying.

He gave an exclamation of impatience. 'Still the school-girl? Did your vigneron never touch you, Christine—never wake you to anything more than silly romantic dreams? Haven't you ever faced the realities of love? It's certainly time you grew up.' He stooped and picked up the calendar, crumpled it and tossed it into the wastebasket. 'From now on,' he said, his eyes narrowed, 'we'll take ourselves a little more seriously. No more shirking your obligations. You undertook to play my fiancée, and I want my money's worth. I've looked after you and given you a home and a harbour, and I don't want you weakly speculating that I'll marry Jackie Lester in the end. I know what I'm about ... I shall see you later—when I've cleaned myself up.'

Chris made a face behind his back as he left her, his boots sounding all the way down the hall. But it was sheer bravado. She was shaken. She felt in a panic about herself. Maybe she had not fallen in love with him at all—maybe it was a kind of reaction from her affair with Francis. She went to the mirror and stared at her reflection. He had not touched her lips, and yet they felt bruised. But over her heart, on her water-green dress, there was the mark of his hand—in red dust. She felt guilty to see it there, and beneath that mark her heart still pounded crazily.

The following evening when Burton came back to the homestead, he had Jackie Lester in the jeep with him.

Frith was taking a shower, and Chris, sitting on the end of the verandah, saw them coming up the steps together. She stared, unable to take it in. Burton carried a large travelling case in each hand and a smaller bag under one arm. Jackie had a cream leather vanity case, her blonde curls gleamed and bounced, and her face was raised to his.

Chris felt violently, furiously angry. Her immediate reaction was to rush to her room, throw everything into a suitcase and leave. In her mind she did all this, but in actuality she sat there shaken by jealousy and rage. How *dared* he! How dared he bring that other girl to the house? She felt as outraged as if she were really engaged to marry him and he was betraying her.

'*What can I do?*' was the wild futile question that hammered in her brain, as she watched them go into the house without even looking her way. Yet she was certain that he at least must know she was there. And he had not even glanced at her. She heard Burton's voice, then Mrs Perry's voice, and then Jackie Lester's ridiculous high-pitched chirruping.

'*Let* him marry her,' she thought, her heart thudding. 'Some men will do anything to get what they want.' She made up her mind that she would have it out with him— that she would leave as soon as she could arrange some kind of transport...

In actual fact she did none of this. For while Mrs Perry installed Jackie in one of the spare bedrooms, Burton came on to the verandah. He stood looking down at Christine, the light of battle in his eyes.

124

'I've brought the opposition right into the camp, Christine. And I expect you to put on a pretty good act. You and I are going to show young Jackie that we mean business.'

'You're crazy,' flashed Chris. 'You'll never get Saltbush that way.'

'You'd be surprised,' said Burton. He sat down on the verandah rail and stared at her.

She said violently, unable to keep the anger and hurt out of her voice, 'Why did you do it? Why did you bring her here?'

He screwed up his eyes irritatingly as if he were considering how to answer that. 'Seeing you're my fiancée,' he said at last, his tone ironic, 'I'll answer your rather hysterical question. First of all, she's a very young and very pretty girl, and I've discovered that one of my employees has been paying her a bit too much attention.' 'Paddy,' thought Chris, far from mollified by his little description of Jackie. 'He doesn't want Paddy to marry her and get hold of Saltbush Flat. So it *is* diplomatic to bring her here.'

'Secondly,' said Burton, 'you complained the other day that Jackie never saw us together. From now on, she's going to. Understand—sweetheart?'

Christ swallowed hard and looked away. 'She's not going to hand over her property to you just because—because— Well, I just don't see how you can win any points that way.'

'No? Well, I've thought it all out carefully, and I can win quite a few points for myself, one way and another. You'll just have to trust in my judgement, and remember *I'm* running this show, not you. I shan't subject you to an embrace right now. I've been, as you observed last evening, riding in the dust all day——'

'Most of the day,' corrected Chris.

He looked at her for a moment, a dangerous smile hovering at the corners of his mouth. 'Most of the day,' he agreed pleasantly. 'I'll take a shower and then we'll get down to business.'

Jackie, that first night at dinner, behaved like the little

queen of the home. Chris was sickened by her sugary, little-girl gratefulness to Burton, and by his bland and smiling acceptance of her effusions.

'It's just *heaven* to be here. It's like—like being in the first real home I've ever known. You wouldn't know what it's like to have only one parent most of your life,' she told Frith and Christine with total disregard for the fact that she knew nothing about either of them. No one corrected her misapprehension, but Frith and Chris exchanged glances, and Burton looked at Jackie with the sort of fond and tolerant amusement that one would accord to a nice child. Or so Chris thought. 'It was so lonesome out at Saltbush Flat, even though I was determined to make it *home*. Wasn't I, Burton?'

'You certainly were,' he agreed.

Jackie glanced round the comfortable dining room with its pleasant furnishings and the soft lamps glowing from the sideboard and the table centre. 'This I just love. Thank you, Burton, for bringing me here.'

Mrs Parry sat silently throughout that meal. Everyone knew that Jackie had what Burton wanted and that she was being quite unco-operative about parting with it, and the way she so blandly played the innocent was astonishing, at least to all the women present.

Burton disappeared to the office after dinner, and the three girls took their coffee to the verandah, and Frith asked flatly, 'What are you going to do about Saltbush Flat now you aren't living there, Jackie?'

Jackie widened her round blue eyes. 'Oh dear, I really don't know! I shall have to talk it over with Burton.'

'You have talked it over with Burton,' said Frith realistically. 'You've put some absolutely crazy price on it and you know perfectly well he won't fall for that. What's the idea?'

Jackie refused to budge from her position of injured innocence. 'You don't understand, Frith. My land's worth a fortune. There's oil or something in all those bores. My solicitor said I'd be silly to sell it just as grazing land.'

'Did he?' Frith was sceptical. 'Then why don't you put it on the market and see how many takers you get?'

'Because—because I want *Burton* to have it.'

'Then why don't you be done with it and make him a present of it?'

Jackie's little round face was screwed up as if in puzzlement. 'It's easy for you to say that, Frith, when you've always had absolutely everything. But I haven't, you see. Mummy and I have had to battle—always. Things have changed for her now she's married again, but that's made it harder for me. I can't intrude on her marriage—I have to support myself—I have to think about that.'

'Why don't you try work?' suggested Frith coldly.

Jackie said slyly, 'Christine and I aren't clever like you, Frith. We're—we're home-makers, aren't we, Christine?'

Chris said unco-operatively, 'If I were you, I know what I should do. I should sell Saltbush Flat to Burton.'

'Maybe you would, Christine. And I know what I'd do if I were *you*. I'd get married as fast as I could. I shouldn't be able to wait to marry a man like Burton. But I just don't think either of you can be all that keen.'

Frith got up. 'Excuse me if I depart,' she said distinctly. 'But I think you are plain bad taste, Miss Jackie Lester. That wide-eyed innocent look of yours doesn't fool me. I happen to know you've been playing round with the overseer.' She stalked off, and Jackie said, 'I just don't know what she means by *that*, do you, Christine?'

Chris said tiredly, 'She saw Paddy Preston kissing you.'

'It was only fun. And because I was getting lonely. And because—well, I thought it wasn't fair to you to be seeing so much of Burton and thinking about him all the time.'

'Then why on earth have you come to Red Sands?'

'Burton just didn't give me any chance. He told me to pack my things and come.' She gave a sudden little spurt of laugher. 'Oh, I think he's an absolutely fabulous man! The awful way he's playing us off against each other! I love him! I can't help it.'

Now it was Chris who got up and walked away. If she'd

stayed, she'd have done something she'd have been sorry for. So she went to bed and missed Burton when he had finished in the office, and they didn't after all get down to business, as he had put it . . .

Nobody at Red Sands liked Jackie. Nobody but Burton, who seemed to find her cute and amusing, and maybe more than that. Dan Spencer was hardly ever seen at the homestead now that she was there, the little boy Jason would not even speak to her, and Mrs Perry called her 'Miss Lester', and treated her as if she were a chance—and very temporary—guest.

Jackie's reaction was to tell Chris with a shudder, 'I can't stand that pudding-faced old thing sneaking round and checking up if I've taken any of the bed linen or set fire to the curtains or something. She gives me the creeps. Anyone can see she's just jealous—she's just so madly enamoured of Burton, she'd lie down and die for him. It's really pathetic.'

Chris said coldly, 'I agree with what Frith said about you, Jackie. You're bad taste.'

'Burton doesn't think so,' said Jackie smugly. 'I can make him laugh, anyhow, which is more than you can.'

Her advent at Red Sands was certainly the start of a different order of things. Chris's fighting spirit was roused despite herself, and she even became a little possessive of Burton, but Jackie seemed unconcerned. While no date had been set for the wedding, she was happy to discount the engagement and to fight with no holds barred. It infuriated Chris the way she continually pointed up the fact that Chris had nothing, whereas she had Saltbush Flat. Each evening, she assumed her innocent little girl air as she welcomed Burton home, sometimes even standing on tiptoe to kiss him. She fussed over him and brought his iced beer or whisky into the sitting room—performing little tasks that had always before been performed by Mrs Perry. Chris cursed herself for not getting in with that first, then adopted the tactics of waiting for Burton and accompanying him into the sitting room and exclaiming, 'Oh, Jackie, how sweet of you to take all that trouble!' She suffered Burton's public and inoffensive kisses, let him put his arm around her waist and responded to his loving looks across the table. Or she presumed they were intended as loving looks. They were certainly long and lingering glances, and several times she found herself caught up by them far too publicly.

Frith, after her initial burst of hostility, proceeded to act as far as possible as if Jackie were not there, and Chris thought that one thing at least satisfied her. While Jackie was at Red Sands she was not seeing Paddy Preston. Chris wondered quite a lot about Paddy—and Frith.

Her own first encounter with Paddy did not come about until one particularly hot evening when she went alone to the waterhole to swim. That was on a bad day after a bad night.

CHAPTER SEVEN

On that bad night, Chris had dutifully put up a good performance of the engaged girl at dinnertime, but afterwards, when Burton suggested they walk in the garden, and out in the darkness drew her into his arms, she panicked suddenly and escaped him. She had no intention of becoming used to Burton's embraces. They were a far more powerful drug than Francis's had ever been, and she knew she was crazy, but she had begun to dream about him and had to keep constantly reminding herself that she was merely being used.

'How's your heart's convalescence, Christine?' he mocked.

'It's fine,' she flashed. 'I'm just about ready to take off. I know I'll be leaving you in good hands.'

He looked at her hard, his eyes calculating in the starlight. 'What's that supposed to mean?'

'As if you don't know! You want Saltbush Flat and there's obviously only one way you'll get it—and I don't think it's such a distasteful way to you, either. You'll take to—to marriage with Jackie Lester like a duck to water.'

He laughed briefly. 'Can't you do better than that with your similes? Anyhow, quit worrying your head about it, there's a good girl. I'll do the thinking. You're here to convalesce, and never fear, I'm cashing in on your convalescence in my own way.'

'Then if I say it's over—that I'm ready to go——'

'I shall want a blueprint of your plans. You can't sign yourself off as easily as all that. I like to see a job well done. Besides, while you shy away from me the way you do you're not well, Christine.'

'Aren't you flattering yourself?' asked Chris.

'I don't think so. A girl of twenty who is a healthy girl likes to be kissed by almost any personable male.'

'How wrong can you be!' exclaimed Chris, incensed. 'And I thought you said you understood the female mind—*my* mind!'

'Meaning you're different from other girls? Superior?' His eyebrows tilted. 'Well, I'll grant that you are, in some respects. You have singularly good looks—a beautiful skin, lovely eyes, except that they're sometimes too wary and evasive. Your mouth leaves nothing to be desired, and your figure is—exceptional.' His eyes roved down the length of her as he spoke. They had wandered back to the path, and light from the house fell in a shaft through the cedar trees on to the paleness of her dress, the redness of her hair.

Chris, unnerved by some seductive note in his voice, asked quickly, 'Is all this to nourish my morale? But you've made one noticeable omission, and I must draw my own conclusion from that.' She tossed back the hair from her shoulders, remembering a phrase he had once used—'for those who like redheads'.

He caught her implication immediately.

'You're talking about your red hair. Well, I wasn't enumerating the things *I* like about you Christine,' he said

130

dampeningly. 'I was merely pointing out some of the ways in which you're exceptional. There are not many girls who have such a formidable array of attractive qualities.'

'I don't want to be admired for my purely physical qualities,' said Chris, disconcerted and aggressive.

'I'm sure you won't be,' Burton said consolingly. 'Not when you grow up. What did Francis like best about you?'

The question was unexpected and left her floundering. She wondered, what *had* Francis liked about her?—not that it was any of Burton's business. Looking back, she seemed to herself to have been so young and gauche, in the days when she loved Francis. Little more than a schoolgirl. Yet Francis had never complained—had never seemed dissatisfied with her youth and inexperience. Now she wondered a little why not...

'I'll make an educated guess,' said Burton after a moment, His eyes were intent on her. 'I think he liked your innocence. He certainly left *that* exactly as he found it. And you're hanging on to it like mad, Christine—like some starry-eyed girl with a pressed flower. Well, I suppose you must keep treasuring it if it pleases you so much.'

He left her abruptly then, and she went to her room feeling shaken to the core, and not caring in the least that Jackie had watched her come in alone. She was wakeful and restless all night, thinking about the past, seeing her love affair with Francis with completely new eyes. It *had* been innocent—very innocent. They had kissed often, but she had never known what it was to be passionately stirred until Burton held her in his arms.

And that was wrong, because Burton was only playing with her.

The next day was burningly hot. Frith disappeared for the day and Jackie had Chris almost at screaming point with her babbling little girl act, and her talk of what Burton had said last night when Chris went early to bed because of a quarrel.

'What was it *about*?' she persisted, and Chris knew she thought it had been about herself and said furiously,

'Haven't you ever heard of a lovers' tiff? Burton doesn't like little lapdogs who are always docile and subservient and—and stupidly ingratiating!' Jackie, hurt, was at last silenced, and Chris felt absurdly ashamed of herself and retired to her room to read and to doze.

Then, late in the afternoon, she went down to the water-hole. She half expected to see Frith there, but instead she encountered a man—a lean dark man with a deeply tanned, slightly haggard face and a wide mouth that was either cruel or sensual or perhaps both.

She had tossed off the cotton shirt she wore over her bikini, kicked her feet free of her canvas shoes and slid into the water without even knowing that he was there. It was a deep waterhole, and the water was clear with an almost green translucence. The heat of the day had been sizzling, and the touch of the water was soft and silky and almost lukewarm. Chris submerged completely, came up tossing her hair from her face and aware of a sort of physical bliss. It was then, as she pushed back her streaming red hair, that she saw him standing on the bank watching her.

A shock of sheer fright went through her. She had no idea in the world who he was, but there was something totally unnerving about the way he stared at her. She simply could not swim about in the water while he was watching her. She got back to the bank and hauled herself out of the water near her clothes, but before she could reach for her shirt he was beside her. His hands, brown and hard, went around her waist and she felt their rough warmth harsh against her cold flesh.

'Don't tell me you're Christine?' he said. He wore a black shirt and narrow drill trousers, and his dark eyes, looking intensely and glintingly into hers, were worldly and knowing, and somehow wicked. She twisted away from him.

'Yes, I'm Christine.' She wished vainly that she had stayed safely in the water. 'Please let me get my shirt.'

He released her, stooped and snatched it up, holding it out of her reach. 'You have too pretty a shape to hide it. A figure like that is meant to be seen and admired.'

Chris, her cheeks red, glared at him furiously. 'Who are you? I'll——'

'You'll tell the Boss? Okay, you do that, but he won't be at all surprised. I'm Paddy Preston—make a mental note of the name. And if you want your shirt you must pay for it. Just a kiss. You'll enjoy it——'

'No!' exclaimed Chris, outraged and afraid to run for it, for there was nowhere really to run to, and besides, he would catch her easily.

His wide mouth smiled and his taunting eyes took in her full length.

'Oh, come on now, don't act so old-fashioned. You can't be that way, or you wouldn't wear a bikini.' He dropped her shirt and reached for her, and though she dodged he caught her and drew her gasping and struggling and helpless against his lean muscular body. His clothes were harsh against her skin, and he tangled one hand in her long hair to hold her captive. Chris, fighting singlemindedly to be free of him, was only vaguely aware of the sound of a horse galloping. There was a heavy thud as the rider leaped to the ground, and then she was released so suddenly she staggered. Her head felt as if her hair had been dragged out by the roots, and Paddy Preston was rolling over and over down the bank towards the water. She stared helpless, open-mouthed, and at the last moment he scrambled to his feet, lurched, and caught his balance. His hand went to his jaw where he had evidently been struck, and Chris turned at last to her rescuer.

It was Burton, grim-faced, narrow-eyed.

'Lay a finger on that girl again, you filthy swine,' he lashed out, 'and I'll whip you off the place! In fact, you'd better get out right now until I've cooled down and then I'll let you know whether or not I want you back!'

The other man shook his head as if to clear it. He looked neither cowed nor embarrassed. In fact, Chris thought he appeared highly stimulated and even on the edge of laughter. He said with wry humour, 'Don't take it so seriously.

It's the satyr in me. I only wanted to kiss your dryad, Burt. I guess I'm sex-starved.'

'And I guess you're over-sexed,' said Burton grimly. 'Are you all right, Christine?'

'Yes,' she said, her voice low and troubled. She had found her shirt and put it on, wrapping it around her body and shivering slightly. There were red mud stains on it and she felt she must look a ridiculous figure. Paddy Preston stood, legs astride, thumbs hooked in his belt, his bright eyes going from her to Burton and back again. She thought suddenly, 'There is something terribly attractive about him —but not for me.' She was thankful Burton had come, but hated the fracas she was causing. Higher up the bank under a tree, Burton's tall black horse stood like a statue. It was an unreal scene. High above, the sky was paling to a curious kind of green, and out on the horizon a flush of pure and stunning red spread like a strain, colouring the vast plains below dramatically.

Chris said, 'He—Paddy—was only trying to kiss me.'

Burton's eyes raked her. They seemed to see right through the absurd shirt to the scanty bikini. He said coldly, 'I don't care to have my girl kissed by a stockman when she comes to swim at the waterhole. I mean what I said, Paddy. You can clear out to the town tonight.'

The two men stared at each other, and Chris was struck by a peculiar feeling that they liked, and even admired, each other. She was aware too that Burton was furiously angry about the situation.

Paddy said laconically, thoughtfully, 'Okay. Right now that might be the best idea, Burt—before I do something really regrettable, one way or another, and you throw me out for good. But see what you can fix about Saltbush while I'm away, will you? Now you've got that girl under your eye at Red Sands, I can see no reason why we shouldn't move the stock back there. She'd never know the difference. We should never have shifted them in the first place, in my view.'

'I know that. But we'll use Saltbush legitimately or not

at all,' said Burton tersely.

'Time's getting short,' Paddy warned. Burton had absently produced cigarettes and he reached across and took one, found his own matches, lit first Burton's cigarette and then his own. Chris found the whole performance incomprehensible—a mixture of hostility and mateship of the most casual kind. 'D'you still want me off the property, Boss?'

'Yes, I do. Get it out of your system, for God's sake.'

Paddy drew on his cigarette. 'All this messing about while the beef loses condition. You should do something about it, Burt, you really should. You're getting soft.' His eyes, dark and faintly malicious, rested on Christine. She felt, shocked, that she was being treated by Paddy as something slightly less than human—as something less important than cattle, or 'beef' as he put it. And she thought, 'He means, of course, why doesn't Burton go ahead and ask Jackie Lester to marry him.' That, obviously, was what *he* would do. There was a ruthlessness, a hard intractableness about him that seemed to leave no room at all for tender feelings. It made her reassess her speculations about Frith. Frith could not possibly be in love with a man like that—basic, fundamental, raw. Undercivilised. A man who belonged here in the red sandhill country and nowhere else. She could not imagine *him* fitting into city society as Burton did. Paddy would have one image only and this was it—that of the outback cattleman, rangy and muscular and tough. 'I'd want more from a man than that,' mused Chris. 'A little culture, a little sensitivity.' Burton had both—with his music, his easy adaptation to the city and its ways.

She glanced through her lashes at the man himself, standing near her now. Dusty, his eyes screwed up, his thumbs stuck in his belt just as Paddy's were. And he had just knocked his overseer down and as good as given him the sack! It was—incredible. And it was wonderful. Chris didn't know why, but it was so. She loved what she saw, was infatuated by it—even by the hard line of his mouth, the grim look in his eyes as he thought about his 'beef'. She thought, 'But *I* know there is another side to him when I need it.' Just as if, she realised with a shock, she really was his girl.

Which was what she wanted to be.

Yes.

Both the men smoked in silence a little longer. Chris was convinced that she had been forgotten. Then Burton said slowly, 'I'm not getting soft, Paddy. But it can wait a little longer. The situation's not desperate yet.'

Paddy, who had produced his hat from the fork of a tree, put it on his head and tipped it back. 'You're making a mistake this time, Boss,' he said. 'You're going to have to move that stock somewhere—and soon! Long Bore won't hold them unless we get rain.' He spoke as if he were on an equal footing with his boss. 'Well, keep in touch. If you want that mob remustered and put on the move, send a smoke signal and I'll be here.' He grinned at Burton, told Chris 'Good luck', and strode off.

Chris saw him go with a feeling of unease. Now she was alone with Burton she felt very, very uncomfortable. She didn't know what was going to happen next.

Burton cocked his brow enquiringly and looked at her almost quizzically. He waited as if some explanation were due from her, and she thought she saw amusement way back in his eyes—sardonic unkind amusement. What a fool she must look in her shirt!

She plunged thoughtlessly into attack.

'Did you have to do that—send him off the place? Will you take him back?'

'I'll consider it,' he said with a lop-sided smile. The sun was flat to the horizon now, and the red glow was spreading out towards them in a soft flood that lit both of them theatrically. 'I'll admit I'm surprised at you, Christine. I never thought to catch you out like that.'

For a moment Chris was speechless. Then—'You can't have listened to all you were told in Adelaide,' she retorted. 'No good can be expected of *me*, you know.'

He smiled an aggravating, tilted smile. 'Don't try to

make me swallow *that*. It's not been my experience of you. And don't try to persuade me that a cold-hearted innocent little pigeon like you has been throwing herself blindly at someone as obvious sensual and hungry as Paddy Preston.'

Chris said, her chin up, 'You were telling me only lately that most girls of my age are only too glad to be kissed by any personable man—you were complaining about my innocence——'

'I wasn't urging you to look elsewhere for someone to deprive you of that,' he said ironically, and Chris reddened.

'And I am not cold-hearted,' she countered, nettled by his description of her.

'No? Then prove it to me. First-hand knowledge is the best.' He dragged her into his arms and his muscles were harder than Paddy's the long length of his body, and his lips were hard and forceful against her mouth. She felt herself sinking into a state of physical delight that she could not struggle against. She returned his kiss, mindless, helpless, blind . . .

And this time it was Burton who drew away first.

'Is all that ardour on my account? Or can I thank my overseer for softening you up?'

Chris gasped. Colour flooded her cheeks and she moved abruptly away and began to search for her canvas shoes. The ground burned with a red light and the shadows were purple, and she hardly knew what she was doing, as the blood pounded madly at her temples.

Burton stooped beside her. 'Just how innocent are you, Christine? Just how innocent do you want to stay? What's been happening to your fixation on the past?'

'I'm looking for my shoes,' said Chris furiously. 'I want to go home.'

He actually laughed, and it had a kindly sound that maddened Chris more than derision would have done.

'Then come home, Chris. You can look for your shoes tomorrow.'

She rode in front of him on the black horse and her feelings were hopelessly jumbled. She was madly in love with him, but she kept remembering what he had said. 'I'm not getting soft, but it can wait a little longer.' *What* could wait? The moment when he told Chris it was all over? And meanwhile he would continue to play around with her heart, would he? She wondered why—and if he knew the devastating effect he was having on her emotions.

'By the way,' he said, when they had reached the horse yard and he had helped her to dismount, 'don't take too much notice of Paddy Preston's flattering attentions, will you? He kisses every girl he can get his hands on.'

'I rather thought he did,' said Chris, trying to sound dignified but all too aware of her ridiculous garb and of the fact that the gravel was none too kind to her bare feet. 'But *I* wasn't taking all that much notice of his kisses. I thought *you* were the one who was doing that.' She saw the fury in his face as she turned to make her getaway and felt a surge of satisfaction that was only spoiled by the fact that she had to hobble rather than run...

Next mail day, two letters of note arrived at Red Sands.

Chris had wakened to a day like any other and come on to the verandah to breakfast with Frith. They were usually alone at the breakfast table, for Jackie got up late, after having a tray brought to her bedroom. Frith looked up from her coffee and said, 'Paddy's coming back today. Burton wants the sale cattle at Long Bore remustered. He must be going to move them to Copper Burr after all.'

She looked happy, and Chris thought, 'For her the day is special.' In her mind, she saw Paddy's face again, the cruel sensual mouth, the wicked laughter in the dark eyes, the toughness of the personality. And she looked at Frith, with her poise and her silvery hair, and her talent for drawing—for she had that, no matter how much she protested. It just didn't make sense to think of Frith and Paddy together...

'I wonder *why* Paddy took off when he did,' said Frith musingly. She finished peeling a freshly picked orange and looked out into the garden where the heat was already beginning to make the flowers droop. 'Was it his idea, or was it Burton's? Sometimes I think Paddy should try to make a

138

go of it away from here—on his own.' She ate a segment of orange thoughtfully. 'I rather suspect Burton knew he'd been making passes at Jackie Lester, and I can think of two reasons why he wouldn't like *that*. One is, he doesn't want Paddy getting ideas about grabbing Saltbush Flat for himself, and the other is that he's got his eye on Jackie himself.' She looked up and caught Chris's eye and reddened guiltily. 'Heavens, what an awful thing to have said! I'm sorry, Chris——'

Chris shrugged. 'Don't worry. It's true enough, and I know it as well as you do, Frith. Maybe even better. Those pastures mean just about everything to Burton and he's got to get them some way.' She turned the conversation quickly. 'But I don't really think Paddy would interest a girl like Jackie. He would be too tough and inconsiderate for a girl like that.'

Frith stared at her. 'How do you know, Chris? I didn't think you'd even met Paddy.'

'I met him once—at the waterhole. I was with Burton,' said Chris, stumbling over the half lie.

'What did you think of him?' Frith leaned her elbows on the table and looked hard at Chris, an almost fanatical expression in her eyes.

'How could I have an opinion after so short an acquaintance?'

'Still, you have. I'd like to hear it. Come on now, be honest.'

Chris groped for words. 'I thought that he's a man who belongs here—just as much as Burton does, maybe even more. The cattle run is his whole life——'

'Yes.' Frith narrowed her eyes and somehow she looked more than ever like the girl in the photograph, her mother, Amy Alexander, who had been frightened almost literally to death by the outback. 'That's fair enough as far as it goes. But Paddy does have another side. He can't, it seems, leave any girl alone. Except me,' she added bitterly. 'He likes women—but not as personalities. Just as—as female flesh.'

It was in some degree what Chris had thought, and yet when Frith said it it seemed wrong. And if he left Frith alone—an attractive girl like Frith——

She looked at Burton's half-sister and shook her head slightly. 'I wouldn't know what to say about that.' She rose from the table. 'I think I'll wash my hair this morning.' It closed a conversation that was becoming too awkward.

And that was the day the two letters came in the mail.

One was an invitation, addressed to Chris, but including Burton. An invitation to a family party at the Gilcrists' Riverina vineyards. Christine Vance and her fiancé, Burton Alexander. The occasion—to welcome Francis Rogeon into the family. Chris was surprised at how little it mattered. Of course she would not go. She glanced at the calendar on a small table in the sitting room and realised with a shock that it was Francis's wedding day. And she had forgotten all about it! She had not wakened with a feeling of dread as she had thought for so long that she would.

As the mail was always distributed by Burton himself, it was after dinner when she received her invitation, and she decided not to mention it. She glanced at him furtively across the sitting room where he too was reading a letter. And that was when she saw the second letter of note. It was in a pink envelope, and even from here she knew that it was scented. Chris remembered he had received a letter just like that soon after she first came to Red Sands, and he had smiled to himself over it then just as he was doing now. She thought with a shock, 'There's a third woman in his life.' She wondered if any of the others knew. Frith was avidly reading letters from Adelaide, and Jackie, who didn't have any letters but had received some fashion magazines, was curled up kittenlike in a chair, looking provocative and picturesque just in case Burton should glance her way.

Chris sat perfectly still, trying to read the expressions that moved across Burton's face as he read that scented, very feminine letter. She wondered dismally, 'What am I fighting for?' She felt suddenly exhausted. She *had* been fighting—she knew it now—to win Burton from Jackie Lester.

And Jackie was so right—*she* held an ace in her hand. It was an unequal battle, especially as Burton was not even remotely in love with Christine Vance. But the woman who wrote the pink letters—where did *she* fit into it all? Chris felt tears rush suddenly to her eyes. It was all so hopeless, so futile. She longed to be able to creep away and cry long and quietly by herself.

Burton, however, chose that moment to look at her. He folded the small pink pages still keeping his eyes on her and asked her in the intimate voice he often used for what Chris thought of as their public—Jackie mainly, but also Frith—'May I see that invitation of yours, Chris? I noticed it when I was sorting the mail.'

Chris bit her lip. She knew that tears unshed were making her eyes overbright, but didn't want to draw attention to them by wiping them away. She said carelessly, 'It's nothing I want to accept.'

He rose lazily and crossed the room to perch himself on the arm of her chair, and casually took the envelope from her hand. Jackie wriggled and sat up and decided to take part.

'Have you got an invitation to a party, Christine? Oh, I just love parties!' No one paid any attention. Frith glanced up briefly, then returned to her own mail.

Burton read the invitation carefully, then looked down into Chris's face. He didn't reprove her for not passing it on. He merely said smilingly, 'Of course you must go. We'll both go.'

'No!' said Chris, appalled. Imagine turning up at a family gathering with Burton! She could not possibly pretend in front of them all to be happily engaged. Burton was glancing at the calendar as Chris had done earlier, and his eyebrows lifted a fraction.

'This is your cousin Pam's wedding day, if my memory serves me right.' His eyes returned to probe hers, to disapprove the tears hanging tremblingly to her lower lashes. Tears for him, though no doubt he would think they were for Francis and all that was past. 'Well, that seems to me to be a very friendly sort of scheme, to have a party to introduce the new member to the whole family. Francis is a vigneron too, isn't he? I should like to meet him. Of course we must accept, Christine.'

'I'd rather not,' said Chris, her voice low. 'It's too far.'

'Nonsense. We shall fly to Griffith and there I've no doubt we shall be met. I see we're invited to stay the night, too. I shall look forward to it, and it will be good for you. Believe me, Christine, it will be very good for you. To have a change from Red Sands,' he added, for Jackie's benefit. Chris knew very well he meant it would be good for her to encounter Francis once more—a Francis now definitely out of reach. She didn't tell him that she couldn't care less about Francis romantically now. Burton had cured her well and truly of her lovesickness. The trouble was, she was now in love with him.

He smiled at her, leaned over and kissed the tip of her nose. And then he went to the piano and played softly, meaningly, that little tune he had played on her first evening at Red Sands.

'Come and sing the words, Christine.'

Jackie was taking it all in with a sharp inquisitive look on her small face, though Frith seemed still oblivious, and mostly to frustrate Jackie. Chris went to the piano and stood slightly behind Burton and sang, 'He is dead and gone, lady, He is dead and gone.' She put her hand on his shoulder and her long red hair brushed his cheek as she leaned forward.

Jackie said at the end of the song, on a long complaining yawn, 'What a horrid dirge! Play something more cheerful, Burton.'

He swung round on the stool and caught Chris around the waist, pulling her down beside him.

'Honey,' he said to Jackie, 'I've a bone to pick with you. When are you going to see your way clear to letting me buy those lovely green acres on Saltbush Flat? I'm planning to move my prize sale cattle soon, and if things were as they used to be, I'd have a choice of two places. Saltbush Flat or, since we've had rain up north, Copper Burr Bore. How about coming out on the run with me in a day or two to see how a cattleman earns his money? The stockmen will be mustering the mob at Long Bore, and you might get a kick out of seeing it.'

Jackie perked up visibly. 'Oh, I would! I'd just love it, Burton. I've been too shy to ask, after all I'm only a guest here, but I'd just love it! All by myself? Just me and you?'

'Just us two,' said Burton. 'And we can have a real heart-to-heart talk about everything.' While he spoke, and smiled at Jackie, he was gently caressing Chris's hip, and it was all she could do not to jump up and run away. Oh, he was a devious man! He could play two girls along with the greatest of ease. *And* meanwhile be receiving love letters from some woman that none of them knew anything about. She could smell the scent of violets and knew it came from the letter he had put in his shirt pocket.

True to his promise, he took Jackie out with him exactly two days later. They were to go in the jeep, and Chris felt the most unbearable pangs of jealousy as they prepared to depart. Jackie was so obviously triumphant at getting him to herself, and appeared at Chris's bedroom door to ask if she would 'do'. She wore a natty little suit of pants and sleeveless top made of pink and white striped cotton. By rights it should have looked like a pair of pyjamas, but it didn't, and with her pink and white complexion, her blonde curls and round blue eyes, she looked quite entrancing. Chris ached with jealousy. It surely wouldn't be hard for any man to succumb to *that*! She told Jackie dryly, 'I'm quite sure you'll "do", but you should ask Burton, not me. He's the one you want to impress, isn't he?'

Jackie pouted. 'I think you're being catty, Christine. I thought we'd agreed to take it in good part. I haven't sulked when you've had all the limelight, have I? I think it's about my turn now.'

Chris opened her mouth to say sharply, 'But you're not engaged to Burton,' then closed it again. Neither was she

143

engaged to Burton. And it seemed almost as if little Miss Goody Twoshoes, as Mrs Perry had once or twice referred sarcastically to Jackie, must know it.

When at last the sound of the jeep had died away, some ten minutes later, Chris wondered what she would do with herself all day—waiting for those two to come home from their heart-to-heart talk. She wondered if Burton would have any success in persuading Jackie to sell out to him, and did not really think he would. Jackie's mind was firmly made up, and she was a girl with an iron determination. One thing was sure enough. The whole affair must come to a head pretty soon. Burton had said not so long ago—to Paddy, that evening by the river bank—that there was no urgency, but Chris knew that time was needed to fatten the cattle, and that Burton was going to lose heavily if he could not give his buyers what they had come to expect from him. Thousands of dollars were involved, and whatever she pretended, Jackie must know that by withholding Saltbush Flat she was upsetting the whole economics of Burton's cattle station.

Frith came in and echoed her thoughts aloud. 'That frightful girl! I wish Burton would take her out into the sandhills and lose her. What wouldn't I give to hear what's going on between those two now!'

Chris, tidying away her shoes and straightening her bed cover, smiled a wan agreement, and Frith continued, 'You must feel even worse than I do ... Look, I have a bright idea, Chris. I've just checked, and there are two motorbikes out in the shed. Why don't we grab one of them and see what we can see at the Long Bore? I'll swear the feed situation's unchanged at Copper Bore—there's been no more rain. Maybe Burton's going to twist Jackie's arm some way.'

Chris hesitated for a moment. Privately, she couldn't see that they would discover anything at Long Bore—apart from Paddy Preston!—and she was quite sure that Burton would be doing the opposite to arm-twisting. However, finally she said 'Yes', because Frith would go anyway, and she didn't fancy being for hours on her own, waiting.

Frith said, 'I'll get Joe to check up on the petrol and so on and meet you out in the yard in half an hour or so. Mrs Perry will give us some tucker, and we'll take a waterbottle. Be sure to wear your hat and a long-sleeved shirt. We don't want to get sunstroke.' She laughed excitedly, and Chris laughed too. She liked Frith, and just now she thought it might be fun to go out to Long Bore. Frith had gone 'almost' there once before, she recalled, so she must know the way.

Half an hour later, she was riding pillion on the motorbike behind Frith, heading away from the homestead through the mulga, with a burning hot sun beating down from a cloudless blue sky. The air vibrated with heat, and clouds of birds scattered from the edges of creek beds as Frith followed the way merrily. Chris thought there must be something of the bushman in her after all, and to some extent relaxed, confident—foolishly, as she discovered later —that all was going well.

CHAPTER EIGHT

It was long past noon, and still they hadn't reached the Long Bore. Both of them were feeling parched and tired. They had stopped earlier to drink from one of the waterbottles they were carrying, and then set off again. They had seen cattle grazing or resting in the mulga, and they had passed two bore windmills. Chris had an uneasy but unspoken feeling that they were travelling in the wrong direction, but with the sun high in a cloudless sky, with a flat endless horizon all around, it was difficult to tell. She had read stories of people travelling in a circle, and began to think she would be more than relieved if the Red Sands

145

homestead came unexpectedly into sight, but of course it did not.

When Frith spied a small grove of trees as they came up a low rise covered with mulga, they made for that eagerly. There was water and the relief of seeing it was great. Both girls were slightly unbalanced in their excitement, and Chris could hardly wait to throw off her shirt and plunge her arms and face into the cool water. The shade of the trees was like paradise, and they sat down on the hard red earth, their backs against tree trunks, eating some of the cold beef and tomatoes that Mrs Perry had provided, biting into hunks of fresh station bread, and drinking iced tea from the thermos. They sat there for a long time, enjoying the comparative coolness, and the relief from the continual bumping over hard ground. Frith seemed thoughtful and disinclined to talk, and Chris wondered if she was worrying about Burton and Red Sands, or daydreaming about Paddy. She certainly looked very weary, and Chris had not the heart to suggest they should press on.

Leaning back, she looked around her drowsily. Under the low-boughed trees grew ham and egg daisies, scented yellow boronia and wild fuchsias with flame-coloured flowers, and up above, Chris could see the intense blue of the sky. It made her think of Burton's eyes. It was a strange blue with just a touch of hyacinth in it, very beautiful, very seductive——

A small twig fell sharply on her bare wrist, and with a start she realised that she had fallen asleep. She looked around her wildly, finding she was alone. Where on earth was Frith? She jumped to her feet, feeling heavy-eyed and stupid, as if she had been asleep for a long time, though it had seemed no more than a minute. She hurried to the edge of the grove and stared out on to the plain anxiously, intensely aware of the hugeness, the vastness of this great cattle run.

There was not a living creature to be seen besides the birds, and, a long way off in a sudden flurry of red dust, an emu running, long-legged and urgent. There were no cattle, no stockmen. No motorbike, no Frith. How could the other girl have sneaked away so quietly, and where—and why—had she gone? Chris walked slowly from the grove, one hand shading her eyes, staring out across the plain, and after what seemed an age, a slight movement caught her eye. It was Frith, who had appeared on the motorbike from a slight hollow in front of one of the low red hills. She came slowly across the plain, and Chris began to wave frantically, for the other girl was going the wrong way.

Chris began to shout, her voice sounding tiny and frightening in the emptiness, and still Frith rode on steadily. She hadn't even looked this way. Chris's heart suddenly stood still. Now she knew what had happened. That silence of Frith's, that thoughtfulness as they had rested—had been because she knew they were lost and hadn't wanted to tell Chris. So while Chris slept, she had gone quietly off to reconnoitre. And now she couldn't find her way back!

'We should never have come,' thought Chris, blaming herself for it all. Burton had told her that Frith didn't belong in the outback. The very thought of Frith lost and on her own was appalling. Chris tried not to think of history repeating itself, tried to discard the idea of aboriginal witchcraft that had crept into the back of her mind, and began to walk firmly and determinedly forward over the red plain that dazzled her with its glare, keeping her eyes fixed on that distant figure on the motorbike moving slowly away through the mulga.

Pretty soon she was drenched with perspiration, her feet were sore and she stumbled several times, tearing the leg of her jeans in some prickly bush. She pushed her hair up into her hat, set her lips, and trudged on. Frith was getting further and further away, and she knew despairingly that soon she was going to lose sight of her. But what could she do? She was helpless.

It was a gust of wind spinning a tumble bush into Frith's way that finally made the girl swerve and by some miracle see Chris. Her frantic waving was indicative of her relief, and Chris felt the scorch of tears on her cheeks as she breathed a sigh of thankfulness.

When at last the two girls were together again, Chris saw that Frith looked totally exhausted.

'I thought I'd never find you again, Chris. I was looking for tracks, and suddenly everything seemed the same. Oh, I thought I was going to die all alone out there! It can happen, you know—I've been warned all my life—never go out alone, never go far except with someone who knows the way. Then when I managed that day—the day I ran into Paddy—I thought I could show them. But I think it was just luck then, or it was because Silver Star knew the way.' Her eyes stared wildly. 'But today we're lost, Chris. Really lost. What are we going to do?'

Chris thought hard. 'To begin with, we'd better get back to the shade of that grove.'

'No!' Frith sounded hysterical. 'Sit there hidden? We'd never be found. We must stay in the open—we must keep moving. That way, we'll be more easily seen. Come on, Chris, get on the pillion——'

Chris looked at her hard, and she was sure that Frith was unnerved beyond the point of common sense. She had the feeling that to argue with her could end in a fight—a physical fight, in scratches and kicks and anything at all. Waste of energy, waste of sanity. And perhaps there was something in what the other girl said. Perhaps they should keep in the open and keep moving. At least they had water. And they would be missed. Burton would come——

Chris climbed on to the seat behind Frith and as they started off in a crazy burst of speed, Frith said, 'If only Paddy would come!'

They hurtled fast across the hard-baked ground, stones ricocheting off the wheels and red dust billowing around them. Chris hung on desperately, sure she was riding with someone demented, someone who rose crazily, purposely, anywhere at all, knowing that she would have to stop the mad flight some way or other and racking her brains how to do it.

Then, as they shot up a long slow slope of sandy red soil,

the motorbike gave a splutter and a whine and stopped of its own accord. Chris thought instantly, 'We're out of petrol.' And it was a thought that proved correct.

They were not only out of petrol, they were also on the edge of the sandhill country. It spread before them, a huge, red, insidious sea, treeless, endless, uncaring. Shimmering with heat beneath a sky that had become brassy and glittering. Under its coating of red dust, Frith's face was ashen, and there was a white line of fear at each side of her mouth.

'The sandhill country,' she whispered, her eyes wide and dark. High above in the glittering sky a huge eagle drifted like a dead leaf, drifted and floated down over the sandhills, seeking for prey. Far away, in single file, four emus ran across a ridge of sand, silently, weirdly, reminding Chris of the cave drawings Burton had shown her. And then Chris almost screamed. Inches from her feet, a heap of whitened bones lay. It was five seconds before she realised they were the bones of a large bird...

What on earth had she been thinking? She tightened her mental control instantly. It was important to stop herself— as well as Frith—from going to pieces. She summoned up a very weak smile and told Frith, 'It's bad—but worse things could happen. We have water, and we have each other. And when Burton discovers we're missing he'll come out in his aircraft and find us.' She sounded far more cheeful than she felt, for she was frightened.

Frith was staring at her blankly.

'We'll light a fire,' said Chris more firmly. She knew there were matches in the picnic box, and there were plenty of twigs and branches about down below the sandhills. She wheeled the motorbike slowly down the long slope and to her relief Frith followed her, and soon the two of them were gathering a pile of stuff for the fire.

'We'll arrange it in two lots,' said Chris cheerfully. 'One we'll set alight and one we'll save for later—if necessary. Then we'll install ourselves among those nice shady trees, Frith, and make ourselves comfortable.'

'Comfortable!' exclaimed Frith with a shudder. 'Aren't

you afraid, Christine?'

'I'll be good and afraid when it's time,' said Chris lightly. She struck a match and hoped Frith would not see how her hand was shaking. She waited till she was sure the fire was going to burn before joining Frith who had already trekked off to some shade, and looked back with satisfaction to see the thick brownish smoke forming a cloud in the hot dry air.

The second fire had been lit and had almost died away when at last they heard the sound of a plane. The whole of the earth was brilliantly red with deep indigo shadows, more unearthly and awesome than anything Chris had ever seen, and she had been staring in silence when that droning came from the sky. In a flash, the two girls had leapt to their feet and were out in the open, waving wildly at the plane that was now circling above them. For a few seconds, Chris saw Burton's face and knew that he had located them, then he took the plane a little away and brought it down slowly, meticulously, to land among the stones and spinifex as close as he dared. Chris watched agonised as it skittered unevenly along before coming to a stop. She saw Burton climb to the ground and begin to walk towards them steadily.

There was a darkness in his face when at last he reached them. He said sombrely, 'Thank God I found you before the sun went! I couldn't have brought that plane down safely once it was dark. What happened to you? Why on earth are you way out here?'

It was Chris who answered, for Frith seemed tongue-tied. 'We were going to Long Bore and we lost the way and ran out of petrol.'

He looked at them both, then, assessingly, clinically. Chris thought they must look a shocking sight, dusty, sweat-stained, slightly tearful. Frith's eyes looked huge and they were swimming with tears, and Chris had to bite hard on her lip to stop her own tears from flowing.

Burton said, 'Are you all right, Chris? Were you afraid?'

150

'Yes,' she said simply, and he held out his arms and she put her face briefly against his breast.

Frith said starkly, 'I thought we were going to die. It was terrible.'

'Die out here? On Red Sands? What nonsense,' said Burton sharply. 'You had wit enough to light a fire. You must have known I'd find you.'

Frith shook her head. 'It was Chris who insisted on the fire. I'd have lain down and died.'

'Don't talk like that.' He put an arm roughly around her shoulder and held her, then told them that he had got through to Long Bore on the two-way radio in the plane as soon as he spotted them.

'Someone's on their way out now with a four-wheel drive. I can't guarantee to get the plane up, and it will be dark very soon now, so we must all three possess our souls in patience and wait.'

It would be Paddy who came, thought Chris, because Paddy, like Burton, must know this country like the back of his hand. While they waited, they drank the hot strong coffee that Burton had brought. It had more than a dash of brandy in it and took the edge of Chris's fatigue away most effectively, and also her desire to weep. Now that night was near, it was chilly out here on the edge of the desert, and it was good to sit close to the fire Burton had lit to guide their rescuer to their whereabouts. Chris felt safe and relaxed with Burton there, and she did not dare to look at his face in the firelight.

That face meant far, far too much to her.

When Paddy pulled up in the four-wheel drive, jumped down and strode over to the fire, Frith was on her feet too, running to him and crying shakenly, 'Oh, Paddy— Paddy——!'

'What a welcome!' he drawled, as Frith threw herself into his arms. Chris saw his wide mouth twist in a wry smile, and she wondered briefly why she had ever thought it a cruel mouth. Right now, it looked bitter, and yet compassionate, as he hugged Frith, his chin against her shining hair. Frith refused to let go of him. She clung to him hard, her arms about his neck, her face pressed to his body. And as Paddy raised his eyes to glance over at Burton, Chris was sure she detected an unusual glitter there. Emotion—from a tough cattleman? Then he patted Frith on the back and said jokingly, 'Don't do that to me, Frith. It's too much for a susceptible male like me. I'll start thinking I'll have to ask you to marry me, and that would be fairly criminal, wouldn't it?—with the outback the tough place it is!' Frith raised drowned blue eyes and stared at him, her arms still around his neck.

A pulse beat at Burton's temple. He rapped out, 'Cut it out, Frith. There's no need to be melodramatic, you're safe and sound now, and you're going to be packed off back to Adelaide this week.'

Frith released her hold on Paddy and swung round, and Chris could see that she had really been crying, and her dusty face was a mess. She said shakily, 'Don't make plans for me, Burton. I'm not going back to Adelaide this week or ever.'

'I'm afraid you are, my girl. The city's the best place for you, and you've just demonstrated it forcefully.'

'*No*,' said Frith. 'There's nothing for me in the city. I want to stay here with Paddy.'

'Don't be a fool,' snapped Burton. 'Just because you're a little upset and you've seen a familiar face——— At all events, that's enough for now. Let's be on our way.'

'Shall I drive?' Paddy asked. His voice was hard, but Chris had seen his eyes as he looked at Frith and put her gently from him. He looked as if someone were cutting out his heart. Surely he could not look like that unless he loved Frith! Chris felt completely bewildered.

Burton said, 'Yes,' and went back to the fire to beat it out. Chris thought he was racked with indecision. Frith clutched at Paddy's arm and babbled, 'Listen to me, Paddy —please! I love you and I want to marry you.'

There was a moment of tense silence.

'Frith,' said Paddy, a deep disquiet in his tone, 'you don't know what you're saying. There must have been too much brandy in that coffee the boss gave you.'

'The boss,' repeated Frith. 'My brother. Don't call him the boss to me.' She began to cry again, all her sophistication pathetically gone, and Chris, waiting in the back of the jeep, felt an intruder on something intensely private. How must it be to love a man like that—or to think that you loved him—and have him reject you? Perhaps to suspect that he loved you and not understand why he should be so adamant. Chris knew why it could be—that he could know about Amy Alexander, but Frith must be completely in the dark. Still, she could not think what had got into Frith—unless it was, as Paddy had suggested, the brandy!

She could see Burton, the glow of the almost extinguished fire lighting his tall form and bowed head, she could see the gold streaks in his hair glowing like metal. Near the jeep Frith stood, her head bowed too, while three feet away Paddy stood silent and unmoving. 'I would never do that,' Chris thought, bitterly hurt for Frith. 'I would never beg a man to marry me, tell him so unashamedly and humbly that I loved him.' She wondered, if she had gone back to Millunga, seen Francis again, would she have humbled herself like that? Begged him to love her again? No, she didn't think she would have, she'd have been too proud. Was that a sign that she had never loved him enough?

At long last they drove through the darkness and eeriness of the outback night, hearing the howl of dingoes, the mournful cry of the mopoke, and somewhere far off the click-click-click-of gilgil sticks, the hollow weird music of the didgeridoo.

That night, Christine and Frith slept under the stars, at the camp at Long Bore, rolled in blankets, with springy saltbush for a mattress.

There, away from the stockman yarning round the fire, with the stars glittering in the sky high above, comforted by hot sweet tea, they talked in low voices for a long time before they fell asleep. Chris could see the silhouettes of two men who sat slightly apart from the others at the camp fire—the man Frith loved, and the man she loved, and she cherished in her heart, achingly, that time of watching and of feeling safe. Cherished it all the more because she knew that it was coming to an end—perhaps very soon.

Frith asked after a long time, 'Did I make a fool of myself, Chris, out there in the sandhills?'

'No more than I did,' said Chris. 'At least neither of us went to pieces. I was really scared—anyone would be. Except someone like Burton—or Paddy.'

'Yes. But I didn't mean *then*, Chris. I know I behaved very badly then—but for you, I'd have gone clean out of my mind. I should have thanked you for that, and I do ... But I meant—about Paddy.'

Chris thought for a long moment. 'No, you didn't make a fool of yourself, Frith. I thought you were very brave to speak up the way you did. And I think the men thought that, too.' She stared up at a sky that looked deeply purple with its scattering of diamond stars, and listened to the quiet crackling of the fire and the low indistinct murmur of male voices. She wondered what Burton and Paddy were talking about now. Were they talking about the situation brought about by Frith? She rather thought not. Men were not like that. They would be talking about cattle—about Saltbush Flat and Copper Burr Bore, and buyers. She wondered if what Burton had told Jackie were true. Could he fatten his cattle at Copper Burr Bore, or was he bluffing? Maybe there had been more rain out there, maybe the ground was soaked and the grass was springing knee-high ...

Frith murmured, 'I don't know what got into me, Chris, I really don't.' She gave a low laugh that sounded weary and sad. 'It wasn't the brandy. The words just seemed to come straight up out of my subconscious, and once I'd started I just went ahead. Do you know, when we were bushed out there and I could see pictures of us dying of heat and thirst and dehydration and so on, I could only

154

think of Paddy. It was Paddy I wanted to come and find us. I thought, If I can see Paddy just once again, I'll die happy. You can't imagine how many times I've come back to Red Sands just to *look* at Paddy. It's about all I usually get around to doing,' she added bitterly. 'Burton keeps tabs on me, though I fooled him this time, learning to ride. But it always puzzles me—why does Paddy let himself be told? He's just not that sort of man. And he was in love with me once—oh, ages ago. It was one spring vacation when I was home—a spring I'll never forget, I was so happy. Then Burton caught us kissing, and oh! didn't the bullwhip roar around our ears! But for the fact that they'd been friends for years and that Paddy is practically indispensable, I think my brother would have whipped him off the property. *I* don't know why. I was terrified, but it was thrilling too. I went back to school the next day and since then'—her voice grew husky, indistinct—'Paddy's never touched me— hardly even given me a civil word. Till this time. And I've chased him this time, Chris.'

She was silent, then Chris asked carefully, 'But why Paddy for you, Frith? You were only a schoolgirl when you had this crush on him. He's not at all your type, really, is he?—a tough cattleman like that.'

'Tough and lusty and earthy,' said Frith wearily. 'And he kisses every girl in sight. Oh, I know it—and I think you do, too. But I don't *care*. Besides, what do you think my type is? Someone nice and reliable like your cousin Richard? Or some city man who's got an interest in the arts?'

'Perhaps,' said Chris awkwardly. 'After all, you're sensitive and artistic, and you do fit into city life.'

'I fit in nowhere,' Frith denied. 'My heart has never found its home. It's like a bird that can't find a nesting place. It keeps flying back to Paddy, however prickly and unwelcoming he is.'

'Perhaps it's the excitement you remember,' Chris said. 'If Burton hadn't made such a drama out of it——'

'No,' said Frith. 'Paddy is my man. I've as good as told

155

him so now, haven't I? I've never given myself away like that before, but at least he knows for sure now how I feel about him. And I'm not sorry or ashamed about what I said.'

They talked no more after that. Frith, exhausted emotionally and physically, fell asleep, but Chris lay wakeful and still in her blankets, thinking about Burton's half-sister. She couldn't make up her mind whether or not he was doing the right thing in putting Frith out of Paddy's reach, for of course he had done that. True enough, Frith had been badly frightened by today's experience—far more frightened than Chris—yet that could be partly due to conditioning. All her life Frith had been subtly warned of the dangers of the outback. Chris knew very well that if *she* had the opportunity, she would settle for Burton and the outback without hesitation, and live here happily for the rest of her life. She was adaptable enough for that, and her love was strong enough for it. It could be that the same applied to Frith, for despite her family background, she was her father's daughter as well as her mother's.

Chris's eyes were closing. 'I shall never have the opportunity to choose the outback,' she thought. It was a thought that she found so infinitely sad she wanted to weep. But she was far too tired to weep. She could feel faint vibrations in the ground, could hear the soft fall of footsteps. She kept her tired eyes closed. Someone stopped near her, stooped and kissed her gently on the forehead. A voice murmured indistinctly, 'My darling Chris'—or she thought it did— and the soft footsteps receded. She opened her eyes with an immense effort and saw Burton tiptoeing away—back to the glowing embers of the camp fire.

Perhaps after all she would have the opportunity.

Perhaps...

Life was almost back to normal the following day. Despite themselves, both girls slept through all the early morning sounds as the stockmen unrolled themselves from their blankets, breakfasted on beef and damper and tea, and rode off to the day's work of rounding up bullocks.

It was a quiet and deserted camp they woke to, Frith with such a sense of outrage and such disappointment that she was almost in tears.

'I had it all fixed to have it out with Paddy in broad daylight. To find out just why he dropped me like he did,' she told Chris as they splashed their faces at a small waterhole where blue and white butterflies hovered, preparatory to demolishing the breakfast of large steaks that the camp cook had prepared for them.

Burton came riding back to the camp soon after they had disposed of steaks, bread and black tea, and told them briskly, 'Right, you girls, get into the jeep and I'll take you back home. You'll have to put up with a slow and bumpy ride—I'm not going to try to get that plane into the air with precious female cargo aboard.'

'I'd rather stay here,' said Frith uncompromisingly.

'Well, you're not going to.' His face hardened and his eyes were narrowed. 'Don't be a fool, Frith. Forget about Paddy—he doesn't want you. What do you think it would do to his life to be saddled with a girl like you? Paddy's not soft like Dan Spencer—he wouldn't uproot himself, go somewhere it was easier to live——'

'I wouldn't ask him to,' flared Frith.

'You'd make the supreme sacrifice and live out here? I wonder how long that would last?'

'You'd be surprised,' countered Frith. 'I think marriage is for keeps just as much as you do.'

She was more like herself as she sparred with Burton. She had been moody and a little sorry for herself, and Chris had thought that hardly boded well for the would-be wife of a cattleman. But now, seeing her with her head up and her spirits roused, Chris wondered again. She was not sure how to assess Amy Frith Alexander.

Burton had barely deposited the two girls at Red Sands homestead before he shot off in the jeep again, his concern now being with his plane and the business of getting it off the ground safely once more. Jackie, who had come promptly on to the verandah at the sound of the car pulling up in the yard, was obviously disconcerted when Burton took off again without a word to her. Frith went straight inside, but Chris, politer and not so downright, caught the full spate of Jackie's grievance, for the little blonde followed her to her bedroom after she had gone to the back verandah to assure Mrs Perry that they were all alive and well.

'Burton sent us the news over the two-way radio last night, dear. I felt upset that I'd let the two of you go off like that.'

'You just couldn't have stopped us, Mrs Perry,' said Chris with an affectionate smile.

'I'll say she couldn't,' Jackie supplemented that as she followed Chris to her room. 'You could hardly wait to get even with me for snitching Burton, could you?'

Chris looked at her in amazement. 'What an extraordinary thing to say! It just never entered my head.'

Jackie was looking her over spitefully. 'Your nose is sunburnt, Christine. It doesn't suit redheads. I'm lucky, I'm a blonde, but I have a skin that tans without the least bit of trouble—if I want it to. But I prefer to stay a fair blonde. Men like us best that way. Frith ought to remember that. She's chasing Paddy Preston, isn't she? Well, she hasn't a hope. If he were in the least interested in her he wouldn't have made such a gigantic pass at me.'

Chris was almost speechless, but she managed to comment scathingly, 'You *are* a fascinating little thing, aren't you? I guess every male within cooee must be ready to come when you whistle. Is that how you see it?'

They stared at each other. Chris was standing in front of the mirror in the dusty, torn clothes she had worn yesterday, and Jackie, in pale pink and white cotton, high-heeled sandals, her hair looking as if she had stepped straight out of the hairdresser's, and her false eyelashes glistening, leaned back in the armchair with its pretty cretonne cover.

After a moment during which Chris felt vaguely ashamed of her rudeness, Jackie said thoughtfully, 'You

158

know, you *could* be attractive, Christine, if you wore the right colours. That coral pink you're always getting dressed up in—someone really ought to tell you it just doesn't go with red hair.'

'Doesn't it?' Chris remembered Burton complimenting her on her choice of just that particular colour. 'Well, suppose you buzz off and work out a beauty schedule or something for me and leave me in peace just now, will you?'

Jackie scrambled quickly to her feet. 'I know you don't really want me to do that, Christine, but it might be a better idea than you think, and when you've left Red Sands you might realise that. It helps, you know, to look pretty and feminine when you're in love with someone.'

She flitted off quickly and Chris was left with a heart that was thudding. She remembered how Burton had planted that kiss on her brow at the camp last night, and the hopes that had sprung in her breast at his murmured endearment. Now she wondered again what had gone on yesterday when he had taken Jackie to Long Bore.

All day, Jackie revealed nothing beyond the fact that she had 'just loved all those fat shiny cows the stockmen were hunting out of the scrub'.

'What a pity you decided to lose yourselves,' she told the other two girls after lunch. 'It was such fun out there. I'm going again soon.'

'Do that,' said Frith with a bright smile. 'Toddle off on your own. You'll get well and truly lost.'

'I won't, you know,' said Jackie smugly. 'I have a very good sense of direction, Frith. And I found an old map of Red Sands in my homestead, so I know exactly where everything is.'

'You think,' said Frith.

But Chris wondered. Jackie, in her opinion, was 'tinny'. And she was a packet of surprises.

'We didn't get round to our business talk yesterday, did we, Jackie?' Burton reflected that night when, dinner over, he and the three girls moved into the sitting room. All the doors were wide open and a pleasantly cool night breeze had invaded the room. The lights were soft and a single moth fluttered perpetually over a pink-hued lampshade. 'I'd like to hear what conclusions you've reached, now you've had ample time to sit and cogitate.'

Jackie fluttered her synthetic eyelashes. The extremely serious expression she had adopted—it was almost solemn —gave her the air of a child dressed as an adult in some charade. She said sweetly, 'It was lovely to see all your cattle, Burton, and I'm really glad you've got such a lot of beautiful grass at Copper Burr Bore. Because——' She paused. 'Well, I should really *like* you to have my place, Burton. I think it would be lovely to have it back in the Alexander family, where it belongs.' She put her head on one side and smiled, and Frith tapped her foot impatiently. Burton leaned back negligently in his chair, his eyes narrowed, a faint smile on his lips.

Jackie said softly, regretfully, 'But you can see my position, can't you? I mean, it *was* a silly price Mr Harrington told me to ask, wasn't it? Of course you accepted it—I don't in the least blame you for that, we're both business people—but there's oil or something there, isn't there? I know you wouldn't bother with it yourself, I don't suppose you'd even give it a thought, but I have to think of myself now, Burton. Now Mummy's married again and I'm all on my own.'

He moved a little and opened his eyes to look directly at Jackie. 'So you do, Jackie, I'll certainly grant you that. You surely are going to need a bit of cash, honey.' He leaned forward, frowned, then went on briskly, 'All right, then. I'm prepared to raise my offer somewhat—not because of the oil, for you've been misled there—but just because you're a nice little kid and I like making people presents.' He smiled meltingly at her, and Chris bit her lip. He certainly had charm, and he could turn it on at will. Maybe he had been turning it on for her more than she had realised, and she had been wallowing in it just as Jackie was doing— her blue eyes fixed dotingly on his face so that she looked, thought Chris unkindly, quite imbecilic. 'Suppose you and I take a trip to Adelaide to see a solicitor and get it all sorted out sensibly and impersonally.'

Jackie screwed up her little round face like a child about to cry. 'I don't want to go to Adelaide, Burton. I don't want to see any more solicitors—they frighten me to death. I'd rather stay here and settle it all privately—with you.'

'I'm sure you would,' muttered Frith, and stood up and paced angrily to the french doors, where she stood with her back to the others, staring out into the darkness. Chris, who could see Jackie digging her pretty little toes in further and further, wondered what Burton would do next.

When he spoke again, his voice was brisk, and Chris thought she detected a note of impatience and irritability in it. 'As you please, Jackie. Dan and I will do a bit of figuring, and I'll let you know what we come up with. How will that do?'

Jackie looked puzzled, her mouth uncertain whether to curve in a smile or not. 'All right, Burton. Thank you.'

Burton left his chair. 'Your parents will soon be home from Japan, honey. You're going to need that money. I'll see Dan now and we'll talk again tomorrow.'

Jackie's face relaxed in a smile. Chris thought to herself, 'She's not going to worry about anything while she's sitting pretty here.' Burton just hadn't won a point, and Jackie's answer to his new proposal was a foregone conclusion. If he didn't realise that, then Chris did . . .

She suddenly became aware that his hand was reaching for hers. 'Come along, Chris. I haven't had a word with you all day.' He pulled her to her feet, kissed her briefly on the lips and with his arm about her shoulders drew her towards the verandah with him. Once they were out of sight of the sitting room, she said fiercely, 'You can let go of me now.'

'Do I have to? I was rather enjoying the sensation of having a more or less pliant female under my hand. That little doll inside is as hard and implacable as granite.'

'She's certainly made up her mind,' said Chris, sounding

faintly amused though she felt not at all that way. 'She wants *you*, Burton. She doesn't care about Red Sands or Saltbush Flat or anything else at all. Only you.'

'So she does.' He looked down at her quizzically in the half dark. 'Do you care, sweetheart?'

Chris forced a smile, but her bones had turned to water at the sound of his casual endearment. 'It's just not my business. I'm sorry I haven't been much of a help to you, though I never thought I could be ... Are you really going to talk to Dan about raising your offer?'

'I think I must.'

'Will she accept?'

'I'm afraid not. But she's going to have every chance.'

Chris moved away from the hand that was cupped over her bare shoulder. 'Then I'd better leave you to conduct your business. Goodnight, Burton.'

She slipped away before he could stop her, and her heart was beating fast. No more kisses, she swore to herself. She might give herself away too completely. And have more to regret, more to weep over.

She went into the garden and paced agitatedly around under the moonless sky, her mind a whirlpool of blackness. She was madly in love with Burton, and she hadn't one hope in a million. As sure as could be, he was going to settle for Jackie. He would never get her off the place in a fit—not until he'd asked her to be his wife. And then it would be only while she arranged her wedding finery ...

There must always be a winner and a loser, thought Chris bitterly, and it looked as though she were destined once again to play the loser.

Late in the night she woke and heard Burton playing the piano—a Chopin Nocturne—and she yearned for him futilely, and shed a few tears.

The next day, he left the homestead early. Mrs Perry said he had gone to Mittagong Dam to look over the condition of the mob that had been brought in from Five Mile Swamp. He had left a note for Jackie, presumably informing her of the figure he and Dan Spencer had come up with in their consultation last night. When Jackie appeared on the verandah in her usual pink, wearing a shady straw hat tied under her chin with a narrow pink ribbon, Frith, who had been sitting in a cane chair staring moodily out across the plain, swung round.

'Well, what do you think of Burton's offer?'

Chris, leaning against the rail and moody too, though perhaps for other reasons, waited for the answer.

Jackie widened her eyes. 'It was quite generous. But I like it here, I really do.'

'What a shame,' said Frith. 'Because no one here likes you.'

'Except Burton,' retorted Jackie, but her cheeks coloured a little. 'I'm going out. Do you think I'll be able to take one of the jeeps?'

'You'll have to ask Dan,' said Frith. 'Tell him Burton said you might—and I hope you get lost,' she finished pleasantly.

Jackie looked at her reproachfully. 'I know you don't really mean that, Frith. But I shan't get lost, I promise you.'

She tripped lightly down the steps and into the garden, and Frith looked at Chris enquiringly. 'Where do you suppose she's off to?'

'I wouldn't have a clue,' said Chris.

She felt that she had been shelved. Everything at Red Sands now centred on Jackie and Saltbush Flat.

CHAPTER NINE

SHE learned where Jackie had been that evening when she was in her room dressing after taking a shower. Jackie knocked and came in looking as if she had just emerged from some air-conditioned apartment where she was waited on by a personal maid. And yet she wore the same pink confection she had sported that morning.

'Too late to make yourself pretty, I'm afraid, Christine,' were her first words. 'You and Burton will never be married now. I've won.'

Chris's heart began a slow painful thumping. Had she been to Mittagong Dam and seen Burton? Was the whole thing over just like that? She felt her legs turn weak as water and wished that she could simply cease to exist—maybe for the next five years. For an instant she wished that she had used her time here to woo Burton, and then she thanked God that she had not. It would only make it all ten times worse. She heard her own voice, cool, sceptical, composed, asking, 'How would you know that, Jackie? Have you been talking to Burton?'

'Not yet. But I shall when he comes in.' Her blue eyes were full of triumph. 'I drove out to the Long Bore today and asked the camp cook to put me on the track to Copper Burr. I had a pretty fair idea of the way because I've made quite a study of that map I found. So I drove on to Copper Burr Bore, and what do you think? It's as dry as a bone! You couldn't fatten a flea on the grasses there. Burton's just been bluffing. He's got to have Saltbush, and there's only one way he can get it.'

Chris looked at her steadily. 'Would you really marry a man who doesn't love you?' She sat down on the side of the bed to fasten her sandals while Jackie hovered triumphantly near the doorway.

'Love? What do you think love is all about, Christine? Of course Burton would love me. He's a *man*, long past the romantic stage and all that soppy stuff. He'll make a wonderful lover, and he's so proud you may be sure any marriage he makes will work. I'll see to that too. I know you think I'm just a silly girl, you and Frith and Mrs Perry, just because I'm little and pretty, but I'm not at all. I've got my head screwed on tighter than you and Frith, and when I've got what I want I'm going to hang on to it. *I'll* keep Burton happy, Christine. I'm mad about him, for a start.'

Chris, listening, believed every word she said and almost envied her her attitude.

'Will you tell Burton you went to Copper Burr to check up?'

'No. I'll just tell him I can't accept his offer. He'll understand.'

She told him, casually and pleasantly at dinner time, and his eyes narrowed.

'You'd better think it over very, very carefully, Jackie. It's my final offer, absolutely. And it would be a very fine fat nest-egg for a girl of your tender years to have.'

'I'm sorry, Burton, you just can't tempt me.'

An oddly ironical smile flitted across his mobile mouth. He said mildly, 'I'll give you till midnight to change your mind. After that—we start all over, right from scratch.'

Jackie nodded solemnly. 'Very well, Burton. I understand.'

His eyes glittered. 'Then if you haven't come to me by midnight, we shall have a long talk tomorrow and get the whole thing properly sorted out before your mother and her husband come back.'

He disappeared after dinner, presumably to the office, and Jackie ostentatiously sat out the evening in the sitting room, reading magazines and listening to the radio. She didn't go to her room until Chris went to hers, with a demure, 'Goodnight, Christine. Sleep well.' Frith had made her departure some half hour earlier, having given up hoping apparently that Jackie would go to the office.

Chris couldn't make up her mind to undress and get into bed. She prowled around the room that had become home to her, now and then standing still to listen to vague night noises. It was a hot and breathless night, the air heavy. Elsewhere, one would think that thunderstorms and rain were about, but not here. Anyhow, rain if it came would be too late here. Jackie had rightly suspected Burton of bluffing, and Chris was astonished that she had managed to drive all the way to Copper Burr and to come back to Red Sands looking as though she'd done nothing more strenuous than go to a tea party. In many ways, she was an amazing girl, and certainly of the stuff from which outback wives are made. And all she had said about marriage to Burton was doubtless true.

'But he deserves better than that,' thought Chris, an ache in her heart.

She had turned out her light and was standing on the verandah when somewhere in the house she heard a clock striking the hour of midnight. Everything was still and no lights were burning except that from the office, and she could see its glow from far along the verandah. As the clock stopped striking, the glow disappeared, a door closed and there was the sound of footsteps coming along the floorboards. In a moment a shadow joined her—Burton. She could feel his weariness as with a sixth sense, and longed to put out a hand to touch him, to tell him she wanted to help. She heard him sigh.

'Still awake, Christine? I hoped you might be. My midnight vigil is over. Jackie hasn't given in gracefully. So——'

Not gracefully or otherwise, thought Chris dryly. So—he had lost the battle.

There was a long silence between them.

When he spoke again it was not about station affairs. Instead, he put his arm about Chris's shoulders and drew her against him, and told her softly, 'I've been neglecting you lately, Chris. Come here and be kissed.'

Reluctant, yet unable to resist, she let him take her in his

166

arms, and she knew for a long moment the sweetness of his lips on hers, the warmth of his body, muscular and strong, against her own. When they drew apart for breath he said quizzically, 'I believe you're really getting over your vigneron complex at last, Chris. It makes me regret I haven't been around a bit more. It could have happened sooner.'

'You've had things more important to do than kissing me better,' said Chris with an effort at matter-of-factness. She added quickly, 'You'll be pleased to know I've even begun to think about a future for myself.' She was ad-libbing and hardly knew what she was going to say next, but the words seemed to come of their own accord, glibly, convincingly. 'I thought I might do nursing. It's useful interesting work, and would give me a roof over my head as well.'

'Was that what you were thinking about out here in the night all by yourself, Chris?'

'I suppose so,' she lied. 'Besides, it's too hot to sleep.'

'You didn't think of me at all? *I* didn't keep you awake?'

'I wondered what was going to happen. You were bluffing about Copper Burr, weren't you, Burton?'

'Yes, of course I was, but Jackie refused to be bluffed. I'd sooner have coped with it that way. But'—he shrugged beside her in the darkness—'I have to have Saltbush some way or another ... About your nursing plans, Christine. I hope they haven't gone further than your head yet. Right now I've a bit too much to deal with, and I think we'll leave you till after the Gilcrist party to welcome Francis, next week. That strikes me as being a good time to decide what's to be done about you. What do you say?'

She thought bitterly, 'What's to be done with Christine.' It was an old problem. It had been Aunt Patricia's once, and Burton had solved it for her. Now it was *his* problem. And perhaps he thought the best thing to do would be to take her back to the Gilcrists and quietly, unobtrusively leave her there. Then he could come back and announce his plans to marry Jackie Lester.

Chris did not like the idea at all. A great impatience rose in her to have the whole thing over and done with.

She said unsteadily, 'We don't have to go to that party, Burton. It's not as if we were really engaged. I'd far sooner we forget it—it would be very easy to make some excuse and put it off.'

'Are you so afraid of seeing Francis again and stirring up old unhappiness and old desires, Christine? Haven't you forgotten yet?'

She shook her head meaninglessly, unable to speak and in the darkness hoping he would not know that there were tears on her lashes. But he put a finger gently to her face and drew it beneath her eye.

'Tears, Christine? I *have* been neglecting you. Come back into my arms.'

'No—please,' she said quickly. 'I'm tired now, and—it's all a bit pointless.'

'Is it? Well, I'm tired too, so I shall let you off. But I shan't let you off that party. We're going, and you can make up your mind to it. You've got to face up to facts, Christine.'

Yes, Chris knew she had a lot of facts to face up to, but they were not the facts he was referring to.

She went to her room and was soon in bed, but lay restless and wakeful. At two o'clock she heard someone walk softly along the verandah, then a door opened and closed quietly. She was sure it was Frith's door and wondered what Burton's sister had been up to—whether she had been meeting Paddy Preston secretly.

She fell asleep soon after that and dreamed troubledly of Burton—of swimming deep, deep down underground in a hidden pool, and of meeting Burton there, swimming too, silently. He reached out and touched her arm and they swam together, then he moved ahead and she followed him up and up, through the green milky water. And then she lost him—and couldn't find her way to the surface. She woke frightened and fighting for breath ...

If Chris was looking pale and drawn the following morning, then so was Frith. Jackie of course would be sweet and dewy-eyed when she appeared, for she believed very firmly in getting her full quota of sleep. Looking in the mirror at her own jaded reflection, Chris thought she was very wise. To look at her, no one would ever think her more than a fluttery silly little blonde, yet here she was, running circles round them all.

Frith suggested a picnic at the waterhole, and Chris, relieved at the means of avoiding Jackie, assented gladly, and they took cushions and cotton blankets with them, with the idea of having a lazy day. There was an excitement beneath Frith's languor, and it was not long before Chris discovered its cause. They had finished their swim and were stretched out in the shade, Chris staring up into the blue of the sky, Frith sitting combing out her silvery hair.

'Paddy came to see me last night. He sent a message with one of the stockmen and I met him out here at the water-hole.'

Chris asked cautiously, 'What was it all about?'

'About us. I was on his conscience after what I said to him the other night, and now at last I know why he's kept clear of me all these years. And he does love me, Chris ... He said he'd always wanted to explain to me, but up till now thought it best to let the affair die a natural death. Seeing that it hadn't—and that he feels the same way about me as I feel about him—he wrestled with his conscience and decided he was going to do what seemed right to him, no matter what Burton wanted.'

There were a few seconds' silence, and then she resumed, 'He told me what happened to my mother. I never knew—I thought she just died when I was born. But apparently she couldn't stand the loneliness here and she walked out into the sandhills and disappeared.' Frith's eyes looked sombre. 'Paddy said my father should never have married her.'

Chris was silent, watching two blue bonnets chasing each other across the water.

Frith said unemotionally, 'It explains a lot of things. Why I'm not called Amy, and why I was sent to Adelaide —and why I was so stupidly frightened the other day.

169

Everyone thinks I'm exactly like my mother, and I'm not—I'm sure I'm not. All the same, I've been given a great big complex about the bush. But I can shed that now, particularly with Paddy to help me.' She sighed deeply. 'You know, Chris, he said that even if Burton hadn't forbidden it, he could never in a million years ask me to marry him for fear I should walk out into the Never-Never and disappear.'

Chris looked at her and she was smiling mysteriously, serenely.

'I'm going to do an awful thing, Chris. Tomorrow, when Dan goes out to the Long Bore with the supplies, I'm going too. And I'm not coming back. I'm going to ask Paddy to marry me—to elope.' She laughed a little. 'He just *must*. We can drive to some little town and get married and confront Burton with a *fait accompli*, and he can do what he likes about it ... Paddy says they won't be moving the stock to Copper Burr—there's no feed there. He says Burton will just have to take drastic action about Saltbush Flat, and the sooner the better.'

'Which means?' asked Chris huskily, her heart in her mouth.

'I don't really know. Paddy says not to worry, Burton can put it all straight as soon as he likes, but he's too soft.'

Too soft, thought Chris. Paddy had said that before. He thought Burton was too soft on her—that he should break his engagement for the sake of his cattle run. What sort of a man was that for Frith to be breaking her neck to marry?

'Well,' said Frith after a moment, 'what do you think of my plans? Are you shocked?'

'Not shocked,' said Chris slowly. 'I think you're very brave, Frith, but are you sure it's what you really want?'

Frith laughed. 'Quite sure. We love each other—and I'm going to take him by storm. I think it will suit Paddy fine—he'd hate a musical comedy sort of marriage. It will be all over and done with before anyone has time to think. Don't you think that's a good start to a marriage?'

They both laughed, but Chris felt uneasy. She shared

Burton's doubts as to whether his sister had the right sort of temperament for outback life.

She had no doubts about Jackie.

That evening, the tension in the homestead was almost tangible. Frith vanished to her room immediately after dinner—to pack, Chris suspected, feeling guilty. And Burton took Jackie to the office with him.

Jackie was really gussied up tonight—in a one-piece pants suit of ivory cotton, with a delicate design of flowers in pink and blue. There was a touch of gold on the tips of her false eyelashes and her mouth was a sweet and luscious pink. Her golden curls bounced as she moved.

Burton said almost formally, 'Will you excuse me, Chris? I'll see you later.'

Chris bowed her head, unable to speak, for her mouth was quite dry. Was she to be told tonight? And was Jackie's and Burton's engagement to be kept secret till after the family party at Gilcrists'?

Love causes pain. The words seemed to burn into her heart. For a mad moment she could picture herself walking blindly out into the sandhills. Anything rather than have to suffer the torment of tomorrow and tomorrow here ... She envied Frith who could do something positive—go out to the camp and ask the man she loved to run away and marry her. Chris thought she would have changed places with Frith like a shot.

She didn't see Jackie again that night, but she saw Burton. She was still on the verandah, feeling terribly alone, when he came with firm footsteps to find her, sat down in the empty chair beside her and groped in his pocket for cigarettes and matches. He said nothing until he had lit his cigarette and then—'Thank God that business is behind me. Something that had to be done. Not something I liked doing.'

Chris waited in a tense silence.

'Tomorrow will need an early start. We'll begin shifting the stock on to Saltbush. Paddy can take the Long Bore and I'll go to Mittagong Dam. We'll have to shelve personal matters for a bit, Christine. Right now I need a bit of shut-eye. I feel as if I'd been dragged through the scrub by a wild bull.' He smiled tiredly and reached out for her hand. Chris's heart was frozen and her fingers were cold. She knew his mind was teeming with station affairs and that he was bone-weary, and she knew that she wanted to weep her heart out. Some crazy hope had lingered on in her breast that a miracle would happen. That he would tell her he couldn't do it—'Because of you, Christine ... Be damned to Saltbush Flat, we'll manage without it even if it means no more butter on our bread.' But Burton didn't love her, and *she* would certainly not console him for the loss of Saltbush Flat.

She said huskily, 'We'd better say goodnight, then. It would never do for you to fall asleep on the job.'

'In one moment.' He carefully put out his cigarette, though it had barely burned a quarter way, and meanwhile he kept his hold on her hand. And then he drew her to her feet and kissed her in a way he had never kissed her before —in a way that made her want to weep again. He kissed her like a man who needs sustaining.

But how could she, Christine, sustain him? She had never had the right to do so, and now she never would. Nevertheless, she clasped her hands behind his neck and returned his kisses—tenderly and without passion.

'This is the end,' she thought, when they parted. 'The last kiss, the last time we shall sit alone in the dark.' She would not let him take her to the Gilcrists'. She could not go through such a fiasco whatever the reason he wanted it—to bolster her ego, to put her to the test.

No, this was the end of the road as far as she and Burton were concerned. The bitter end.

She woke in the morning to a world that had changed. Frith who like everyone else was apparently to be kept in the dark until Burton got Chris safely away from Red Sands, said a gay goodbye to Chris before she went out to the jeep to join Dan, and Chris felt very much alone when she had gone.

Burton had long ago left for Mittagong Dam, and Jackie, when she emerged from her room, looked very chirpy.

'I'm going over to Saltbush Flat to collect a few things I left in the house,' she told Chris. 'I shan't ever have to live *there* again. My parents will be back from Japan in two days, and I'm going to join them for a little while. I want to see something of them before——' She stopped suddenly and looked at Chris with eyes that were a shining blue. 'But Burton has explained it all to you, I guess.'

Chris shook her head. 'Then he *will*,' said Jackie happily.

Yes, Chris supposed that he would, in his good time. He certainly hadn't done so last night. Was he aiming to keep up the pretence even with her until the party? Suddenly it was all sordid and hateful beyond words.

'Yet it is my own fault,' she thought, 'for being weak enough to get mixed up in this business in the first place.' Her eyes had certainly been tightly shut when she went into it. All she had thought about then was herself and her heartbreak, and getting away from her relatives. She had never for a minute imagined that she would forget Francis so completely and fall so hard in love with Burton Alexander. And now it had ended the same way as that other affair.

It was a hot oppressive day, and the sky over the plain was peculiarly hazy and had a sullen reddish tinge about it. In the afternoon she lay on her bed and her mind worked feverishly. Tonight, she and Jackie would be alone with Burton after dinner. It was an unbearable thought. And yet, quite possibly, Burton would have his time and his mind occupied with Frith's departure. She wondered if he would contact Paddy at the camp at Long Bore, and whether by then the overseer and Frith would already have driven off to some little country town where they would be married the next day.

As she lay, eyes half closed, body tense and unable to relax, a wild idea formed in her mind. Why shouldn't *she* go out to Long Bore and ask Frith and Paddy to take her with them to wherever they were going? It seemed to Chris to be the only possible means of escaping from Red Sands station . . .

She suddenly discovered that she had left her bed and was pulling clothes from the cupboards and drawers and packing them. She began to take notice of what she was doing. One pile of clothes to be left here, in her big suitcase, another very small pile to be taken with her in a little zipper bag.

But how on earth was she to get to Long Bore?

The answer to that question was already there too. Oh, the cunningness of the human mind! She would ride White Star, of course! White Star knew the way to Long Bore.

Another five minutes and she was ready to go. She decided not to involve Mrs Perry, but wrote a short note to Burton which she left propped up on the dressing table. 'Dear Burton—Thank you for your hospitality. I hope everything goes right for you from now on. I would rather not stay any longer, for I know I should be an embarrassment to you now that you are going to marry Jackie. I am taking White Star and going to Long Bore to join Frith. Sincerely, Christine.' She had to brush tears from her lashes as she sealed the envelope and wrote Burton's name on it.

It was burningly hot outside. She slipped round the house the long way so that Mrs Perry would not see her go, and in the yard she found Joe, and asked for White Star to be saddled.

'Don't ride far, Miss Vance,' Joe warned her. 'That's a nasty sky—could mean anything.'

'Rain?' she asked with a smile.

'No, not rain. Dust.'

Chris looked anxiously at the sky. She looked out along the track to the north. The dust, if it was dust, was over towards the west. To the north and to the east, the blue of the sky was untainted, pure, singing, beautiful. And that was the way she was going. She said lightly, 'I'll be all right, Joe. I'll keep away from the dust.'

'Easier said than done,' he said with a grin. 'Where are you heading for, Miss Vance?'

'Oh, to meet up with Frith,' she said evasively.

'You're a bit early. Take it slowly, and you might meet up,' he advised. 'And watch it, won't you?'

Chris promised that she would watch it. He didn't ask her what she carried in her little bag, though she thought he looked at it curiously, and she felt a little like Dick Whittington setting forth into the world, but not half so brave or confident. All the same, it was, as Frith had described it, positive action, and positive action is comforting.

She set off at a canter and was reassured to find that White Star plainly knew the track and followed it without any direction from her rider. Soon it was too hot for cantering, and the little horse dropped down to a walk, and Chris felt the sun streaming down on her in all its fierce heat. The glare from the red plain was blinding, but she tried to follow the faint signs of the track to Long Bore. It was not really so difficult, for Dan had passed that way today with the jeep, and though the earth was hard baked, the wheel marks showed here and there in sandy places. 'I'm becoming quite a bushman,' Chris congratulated herself. She watched intently for a long time, taking pleasure in detecting where the jeep had gone and having her diagnosis confirmed by White Star's unerring process.

Then, as heat and thirst caught up with her, depression set in. If this was something of an adventure, it was a far from happy one. This was the last time she would ride over the Red Sands run. And she would never see Burton again. She had tried to avoid thinking of that, but the knowledge was there at the back of her mind, deeply, painfully etched. Chris allowed a few tears to fall. There was no one to see them, and it seemed not to matter. Tomorrow she might be in some dusty little one-horse town, attending Frith's and Paddy's wedding ceremony, and she must not weep then. After that, when Frith and Paddy came back, she would be on her own, completely and utterly, and she would have to think what to do next.

'There'll be a train to somewhere,' she thought. 'Or there'll be a mail truck. Or someone will be going through —to somewhere.' It might be to Alice Springs, she thought, and tried to feel excited. Or to Perth or Kalgoorlie, or Esperance. Even to Darwin, or Tenants Creek. At all events, it would be to some place where she could lose herself and start all over again. Third time lucky.

White Star walked slowly steadily on, and Chris forgot the track and looked up at the sky. It was clear, cloudless, perfect. A holy sort of a blue. A blue that made you think of the Garden of Eden. Following up that thought, she recalled the little lake where Burton had taken her the day they went to the old homestead. The last remaining scrap of what had once been a Garden of Eden, Burton had said. And that Garden—the sacred hunting grounds of a tribe that had all but disappeared. It was a strange, wild, eerie country and Chris realised anew that she knew next to nothing about it, and never would know more now. But this horse, White Star, had been born and bred here, and it was her home. As it was Burton's and Paddy's. As it was once again to be Frith's. As it was to be Jackie's. Her mind, sickened, rejected that thought.

Somewhere, she thought, feeling herself drooping and extinguished by the heat, they would soon have to turn north-east. White Star would know when, would take her track automatically, for Chris was quite certain that the horse knew where she wanted to go and would take her there. When they reached some trees at the foot of a low red range, Chris decided to dismount and have a drink from her water-bag, and if she could find water to wash her face. Besides, White Star must be thirsty too.

There was water among the trees. Chris sprang down from the saddle, tossed the reins over her arm and led the horse along the sandy red bank and left her to drink while she refreshed herself from the water-flask she had taken from the saddlebag. She walked a little way along the bank and found a small rocky basin where the water looked clear

176

and fresh, and there she splashed her face and neck and let the cool water wash over her wrists. How deep the shade was here beneath the trees, she reflected, as she wiped her face on a tissue. So deep that one would think it was late evening. A sudden wild swish of wind made the trees around her dip their branches to sweep the ground, making a blur of green and blue and gold where small clumps of wild flowers grew. Chris looked back, stirred to an intuitive though faint alarm, and saw White Star standing head up, nostrils flaring. Then, in a flash, the horse had pivoted round and was racing out into the open as if pursued by a devil.

'Hey!' Chris's voice was whipped from her mouth by the wind. She too ran for the open and now she could hear the wind roaring. White Star was galloping madly away over the plain, and ahead of her a great column of dust rose into the air and careered along too, like some huge red demon. Chris's heart was in her mouth. She had not a hope in the world of catching that horse, and now it was plain there was a dust storm coming. Away on the edge of the plain dust was gathering in a low spreading cloud, darkening the sky, and blotting out the horizon. A scattering of dried tumble bushes began to roll along ahead of the wind, slowly at first, as if stirring to life, then moving faster and faster till they were madly spinning balls, tearing along in the path of the dust storm. White Star was no longer to be seen, and the mulga was swelling and heaving like a grey endless sea.

Birds flew into the air in clouds, pink and grey galahs, bright parakeets, tiny green budgerigars, black and white cockatoos—screeching in fright or excitement before they settled in the swaying dipping trees. Chris watched in a fearful fascination. The red dust was filling the sky now, whirling, swirling, spinning. The tumble bushes went mad, bouncing and turning, tearing this way and that at the wind's will, and the sun was like a weird copper disc, hazed over in a sky that came down lower and lower. Whirly winds danced everywhere, tossing bits of bark and branches about as if they were playing some unearthly game. And as Chris stared, half hypnotised, the thought came to her that they were the spirits of the Wingealla tribe.

Then, incredibly, she was walking out to meet them. It was as though she were being called. 'Come—come—come!'—as though she too must join in the game with—someone.

'I should be frightened,' she thought, wondering at herself. 'I'm all alone—and I'm lost—completely lost.' Yet strangely, she was not frightened—not in the least little way. Eerie voices, faint whispering that was barely audible, seemed to fill her ears. Chris walked on and on, mindlessly —into the thickening dust. She felt strongly all about her the presence of aboriginals of a past era, an era before the white man came. She was very much aware that she walked on sacred ground, and now the hot, thrusting wind was pressing her to go on—to hurry—to run. It had come around behind her and was nudging her in the small of the back so that her feet moved faster and faster until presently she was walking on the wind—half floating, half flying. But where to—where to?

The wind was all about her and the dust was so thick that she must keep her eyes closed. There was dust in her nostrils and in her mouth, red dust in her hair. She could smell the dust and taste it on her tongue, and she could hear her own voice saying, 'I see dust, Burton. You've been riding in the dust ...'

Then suddenly she felt deathly cold. She had stepped over the edge of the world into nothingness ...

CHAPTER TEN

THE next thing she was aware of was that she was in a cave—a wide, echoing cave. Though how she had got there she had not the faintest notion. She was lying on soft red sand, one arm flung across her cheek. Faint, reddish light filtered in through a long slanting slit in the rock walls, and faintly illumined, she saw a drawing in black and ochre and earth red. It was a drawing of a black man chasing an emu.

Chris sat up slowly, her eyes widening. She was in the sacred cave that Burton had shown her long ago—the Cave of the Winds. It was a long, long way from the Long Bore, and how she had found it she did not know. She only knew, crazily, that the wind from the red desert sands had somehow or other carried her here. She could hear that wind now, prowling around outside, as if it were her guardian and protector. She thought of witchcraft, and the curse that had destroyed two Alexander women. But she, Chris, was Burton Alexander's girl, and the aboriginals, past and present, were his friends, and she was not afraid. The thought had settled in her mind like a white bird of peace. 'They know I love him,' she thought, and remembered how he had said, 'They know the relationship between us better perhaps than we do ourselves.'

Presently she stood up. Her muscles were aching and tired, and her feet felt bruised, but she made her way to the opening of the cave. Outside, the sky was a deep dark red, and it was full of small flying objects—leaves and twigs and bark, black scrawls against the thinning dust that still raced by overhead. She knew that the storm was almost over and that it must be sundown, for the whole of the world was red. The mulga, purple-shadowed, was red, and the bare patches of plain threw back red lights to the sky. Chris stood staring blankly. She was thirsty and she was exhausted—she doubted whether she would be able to walk more than twenty yards. And the winds had gone and left her to herself. She looked down and saw that her hands, her arms, were red with dust. The pale blue of her shirt was stained a soft red, her jeans were rusty-looking. The red ruby on her finger caught a spark of light as she flipped her long hair back over her shoulder.

She thought, without volition, 'I can't leave now. I belong here—it's my country.' She wondered without emotion if perhaps she would die out here—if this was the end. And she wondered if the dust storm had swept all over the Red Sands cattle run. If it had stopped Paddy and Frith from running away to be married, if it had caught even Jackie Lester out so that she had not been able to get back from Saltbush Flat to the Red Sands homestead.

Perhaps they would all be missing tonight—Jackie and Frith and herself. Who would Burton think about first?

'Of me,' was her instant thought. Why not? Jackie would be safe enough at Saltbush, Frith would be at the cattle camp with Paddy. But Christine—Christine was out on the edge of the sandhill country, sheltering in the sacred cave— a long, long way from home.

Presently she returned to the cave and sat down just inside the entrance. The heat of the day was going fast, and when the darkness came, there were no stars. Chris sat and waited, though for what she did not know. As the night wore on she grew cold and light-headed. She had stretched herself out on the ground and every now and again she almost fell asleep. Almost, but not quite. Her thirst kept her awake. And so she lay between sleep and consciousness, and it seemed to her that she could hear a Chopin Nocturne being played, very softly, very beautifully, on an unseen piano . . .

Suddenly she sat up with a start. She heard the click, click, click of gilgil sticks, the droning song of the didgeridoo. And the scent of honey was on the air. Honey possum! And a voice was calling, 'Christine! Where are you? Christine!'

She saw the glow of a swinging lamp, and she saw a man's face.

Burton! Or was she imagining it? She scrambled to her feet, raked her fingers through her tangled hair and blinked hard to clear her eyes. But she could not rid herself of that lightness in her head and she was sure she was dreaming still. She heard herself say in a strange, shaken voice, 'I'm here, Burton. The wind looked after me.'

'The—*what*, Christine? What did you say?' But he was close to her now, examining her face in the light of his lamp, one hand steadyingly on her arm.

'The wind,' she repeated. 'The wind.' She was babbling and she was crying too, and her arms were closing about his waist. She was clinging hard to him and discovering that he was very real indeed. The lamp swayed as he put it down, and then he was holding her in his arms.

'You're near collapse, my girl. Have you been in the sun?'

'In the dust,' wept Christine. 'And I'm so tired—so thirsty.' She was ashamed of her tears and her weakness. She had thought herself so brave, so unafraid. She had thought she belonged to this land. Now she could only think that she might have died out here, and she never wanted to let go of Burton again.

He disentangled himself from her at last and produced a flask of water, and she drank from it greedily while weak tears ran down over her dust-coated cheeks.

'I don't wonder you're tired,' he said, his voice kind. 'Do you know how many miles you must have walked?'

She shook her head and gave a weak laugh. 'A thousand, by the feel of my feet ... How did you know where to find me?'

'The aboriginals told me.'

'How did *they* know?'

'The wind spirits that brought you here told them—so they say,' he said casually.

'It's true,' said Chris soberly, remembering how that wind had pushed and nudged and then carried her. She could not have stayed where she was even had she wanted to.

Burton was looking at her quizzically. 'All right, if you say so, Chris . . . But now I'm going to get you into the jeep and take you home.' He lifted her in his arms and carried her to the jeep, and Christine slept all the way home. Just before she fell asleep, it occurred to her to ask Burton how he could find the way in the dark, but she could not make the effort. And after all, he had got here, so he would get back again.

At Red Sands homestead, Chris opened her eyes to find everything in darkness. She was in Burton's arms once more and he was carrying her along the verandah to her bedroom. There he closed the door, switched on the light, and deposited her in a chair. Then he straightened up and looked at her ruefully.

'You're a very sorry sight, Christine. You look as if you've been made up for a corroboree by somebody with a *very* heavy hand! What am I going to do with you? Put you in between those nice clean white sheets and let you sleep yourself out?'

Chris struggled upright. Reality came surging back. She remembered Jackie Lester, and her own wild plans to get away—plans that had so completely misfired. And she knew she couldn't sleep.

'No, I'll take a shower and——'

'And join me in the sun room for bacon and eggs?' His eyes were kind and searching, and she gulped and nodded.

He left her to her own devices, and when she had showered and was pulling on clean shirt and clean jeans, she was aware of a feeling of defeat. She was right back where she had been before she rode away—with the same problems, the same uncomfortable situation, to face.

A moment later, Burton tapped softly on her door.

'Ready, Chris?'

And then she was sharing a very intimate, very early

lamplit breakfast with him a small room that was seldom used. He commented that she was looking more like herself again, but after that neither of them said anything. Chris, despite herself, was ravenous, and then, when she had finished her second cup of tea, he looked across the table at her, his blue eyes fixed very steadily on her face, and said quietly, 'And now, Christine, suppose you tell me what all this is about me marrying Jackie Lester.' He had taken from his breast pocket the note she had written him, and she felt the colour leave her cheeks.

She swallowed and said brightly, 'Well, I know. You've got Saltbush Flat now, haven't you?'

'So I have.'

He waited, and she stumbled on, 'And Jackie said——' There she paused. What *had* Jackie said? Burton will explain it all to you. She stared at Burton. '*Aren't* you going to marry Jackie?'

'That, Christine, is the last thing I'd do. There's only one person I want to marry, and that's you. I planned to ask you after we'd been the Gilcrists' party and it had been brought home to you that you've really got over that little love affair. For you have, you know. No girl whose heart wasn't in it could kiss the way you kissed me the other night. You've never been much of an actress, my Christine, and that surely was some kiss you handed out.'

Chris's jaw had dropped and her eyes were enormous. He loved her. Her, Christine Vance! She could not believe it. She felt utterly stupefied. She asked dazedly, 'But, Burton —Saltbush Flat—Jackie would never sell it to you. What did you do?'

'I'm afraid I put one over on young Jackie,' he admitted ruefully. 'I didn't want to do it, but there was no other course open to me. I'd given her every chance. You see, Arthur really wanted me to have Saltbush Flat. I think you know that Violet Lester never bothered with the old fellow since she met him when Jackie was three or four years old. So Arthur finally changed his mind, and he changed his will, and he gave the new one in a sealed packet to Paddy!'

'And Paddy *lost* it?'

'No. Paddy forgot it. He turned it up a few days after the funeral. By that time, I'd had a talk with Jackie and her mother and we'd paid our first visit to the solicitor.'

'Then shouldn't you have produced it?'

Burton shrugged. 'It wasn't valid. The witnesses hadn't dated their signatures. There would have been a bit of business to go through, and it seemed kind of mean to do that to a kid who was so delighted with her windfall. At any rate, I'd always wanted to buy the place from Arthur—I never expected it as a gift. So I simply thought we'd put the sale through, and that would be that.'

By this time, by some sleight of hand on Burton's part, Chris discovered that she was comfortably ensconced beside him on a small lounger, and that his arm was very firmly about her. She said, not yet quite relaxed, 'But Jackie fell in love with you, and it wasn't so simple.'

'Exactly. And she was so very clinging that it occurred to me it would be really handy to have a fiancée around.'

Chris made a rueful grimace. 'On what odd things do our fates hinge!'

'Not at all, sweetheart,' he said suavely. 'I'd been turning over ways and means in my mind for a long time of how to keep a hold on you while you were getting through your convalescence. The last thing I wanted was for you to shoot off out of my orbit and never be seen again. You were my girl, and I was determined to have you.'

Chris sat up straight and stared at him indignantly. 'Really? And you never told me!'

'What would have been the use? It wasn't the sort of thing you wanted to be told at that stage, now was it?'

'No,' she admitted. 'But I want to be told now. I was so terribly afraid that you liked pretty little blondes—particularly when they had what you wanted most.'

'You're extremely naïve, my Christine. I like fascinating, beautiful, maddening redheads, who know how to fall passionately in love. *They* are the ones who have what I want most in the world.'

'Oh,' said Chris inadequately. 'But what did you do about Jackie, Burton? Do we have a court case ahead of us? I thought it was all in the bag——'

'It is. Jackie's accepted my offer—quite a generous one, I'm sure you'll be pleased to know. Otherwise,' he said solemnly, 'I told her I would produce a will with a later date that had just now been unearthed by Paddy. I showed her that will, and though she's a sharp little girl, she's not sharp enough to know that it was invalid. But she's a good sport. She took it philosophically, and tomorrow she'll be off to meet her parents, and I don't think we shall see her again.'

Chris hoped not, and she thought Jackie had got far more than she deserved. Yet, paradoxically, she could not help being glad Burton had dealt with the matter this way—generously, fairly. 'One other thing I'd like to know, Burton,' she asked hesitatingly. 'Who were those pink letters from? The ones that made you smile, and that smelled of violets.'

'Can't you guess?' His eyebrows rose and he smiled down at her, the slightly crooked smile that did such things to her heart. 'They were from Jackie's mum, asking me to keep an eye on her little girl. Violet, I'll swear, was hoping I'd marry the girl and by doing so, rid her of a problem and relieve her guilty conscience. You see, Chris'—his arm tightened about her—'besides the will, Arthur left a copy of a letter he'd written to Violet Lester, telling her of his change of plan and the reason for it. So Violet knew very well that I was being cheated, and that, I'm afraid, was the reason I was hurried to the solicitor to get the sale through before she went off to Japan ... Ah well, Jackie will have plenty of money of her own now to get into all the mischief in the world without making a hole in her stepfather's pocket.'

'Where *is* Jackie?' Chris asked after a moment of relaxing completely into Burton's embrace. 'Is she all right?'

'Sure she's all right. Jackie got back from Saltbush Flat on the tail of the dust storm without batting an eyelid.

She's an amazing girl. There she was on the doorstep to welcome me when I came home, curls and eyelashes and pink petals and all.'

'And Frith?' Even now, Chris didn't care to dwell on the picture of Jackie.

'I went out to Long Bore,' Burton said sombrely. 'Paddy told me of Frith's plans to carry him off and get him tied up. Of course he wasn't going to be in that—he told me he wanted to marry her decently and openly and,' he finished .wryly, 'that if I objected I could go to hell.'

'And did you object, Burton?'

His eyes grew troubled and a shadow passed across his face. 'No. It's too late now.'

'You don't think Frith will be happy—and safe?'

'I don't know any more. I rather suspect that Frith has grown away from me. I'm going to have to start all over again getting to know her as she really is.'

'I think it will work out,' said Christine.

'You and Frith are good pals, aren't you? So you may be right and I hope you are. With you here too, I'd say the marriage had a pretty fair chance. Only for God's sake, don't *you* do any more of these disappearing acts, will you?'

'Never,' said Chris emphatically.

He folded her in his arms. 'No regrets about the nursing career, Chris?'

'None. It was just an idea—of what to do about myself.'

'You think my idea's better?'

'Much better.'

'I think so too. You've been quite a weight on my mind. What about the family party? If you don't want to go, we shan't.'

'I want to go,' said Chris simply, her face raised to his. 'Now we're really engaged.'

'You aren't afraid that seeing Francis will upset you?'

She shook her head and smiled at him, her grey eyes clear and honest. 'I don't think I'll ever see Francis. I shall see only you.'

They kissed, and when at last they drew apart the dawn light, rosy and clear, lay softly on the plain and was reflected in their two faces. Burton drew a finger down the curve of her cheek.

'It's a working day, Chris. I shall have to leave you. Promise me you'll be here when I come back.' He spoke lightly, but his eyes were serious and she knew he was thinking of that shadow that had hung over the past.

'I promise, Burton,' she said steadily. 'I'll be here—always.'

FREE!

Harlequin Romance Catalogue

Here is a wonderful opportunity to read many of the Harlequin Romances you may have missed.

The HARLEQUIN ROMANCE CATALOGUE lists hundreds of titles which possibly are no longer available at your local bookseller. To receive your copy, just fill out the coupon below, mail it to us, and we'll rush your catalogue to you!

Following this page you'll find a sampling of a few of the Harlequin Romances listed in the catalogue. Should you wish to order any of these immediately, kindly check the titles desired and mail with coupon.

To: HARLEQUIN READER SERVICE, Dept. N 402
M.P.O. Box 707, Niagara Falls, N.Y. 14302
Canadian address: Stratford, Ont., Canada

☐ Please send me the free Harlequin Romance Catalogue.
☐ Please send me the titles checked.

I enclose $_____ (No C.O.D.'s), All books are 60c each. To help defray postage and handling cost, please add 25c.

Name _____

Address _____

City/Town _____

State/Prov. _____ Zip _____

Have You Missed Any of These
Harlequin Romances?

All books are 60c. Please use the handy order coupon.

JJ

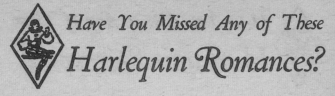

Have You Missed Any of These
Harlequin Romances?

All books are 60c. Please use the handy order coupon.

KK

Have You Missed Any of These
Harlequin Romances?

All books are 60c. Please use the handy order coupon.

LL

Harlequin Presents..

Three of the world's greatest romance authors.
Don't miss any of this new series. Only 75c each!

ANNE HAMPSON

- [ ] #1 GATES OF STEEL
- [ ] #2 MASTER OF MOONROCK
- [ ] #7 DEAR STRANGER
- [ ] #10 WAVES OF FIRE
- [ ] #13 A KISS FROM SATAN
- [ ] #16 WINGS OF NIGHT
- [ ] #19 SOUTH OF MANDRAKI
- [ ] #22 THE HAWK AND THE DOVE
- [ ] #25 BY FOUNTAINS WILD
- [ ] #28 DARK AVENGER
- [ ] #31 BLUE HILLS OF SINTRA
- [ ] #34 STORMY THE WAY

ANNE MATHER

- [ ] #3 SWEET REVENGE
- [ ] #4 THE PLEASURE & THE PAIN
- [ ] #8 THE SANCHEZ TRADITION
- [ ] #11 WHO RIDES THE TIGER
- [ ] #14 STORM IN A RAIN BARREL
- [ ] #17 LIVING WITH ADAM
- [ ] #20 A DISTANT SOUND OF THUNDER
- [ ] #23 THE LEGEND OF LEXANDROS
- [ ] #26 DARK ENEMY
- [ ] #29 MONKSHOOD
- [ ] #32 JAKE HOWARD'S WIFE
- [ ] #35 SEEN BY CANDLELIGHT

VIOLET WINSPEAR

- [ ] #5 DEVIL IN A SILVER ROOM
- [ ] #6 THE HONEY IS BITTER
- [ ] #9 WIFE WITHOUT KISSES
- [ ] #12 DRAGON BAY
- [ ] #15 THE LITTLE NOBODY
- [ ] #18 THE KISSES AND THE WINE
- [ ] #21 THE UNWILLING BRIDE
- [ ] #24 PILGRIM'S CASTLE
- [ ] #27 HOUSE OF STRANGERS
- [ ] #30 BRIDE OF LUCIFER
- [ ] #33 FORBIDDEN RAPTURE
- [ ] #36 LOVE'S PRISONER

To: HARLEQUIN READER SERVICE, Dept. N 402
M.P.O. Box 707, Niagara Falls, N.Y. 14302
Canadian address: Stratford, Ont., Canada

- [ ] Please send me the free Harlequin Romance Presents Catalogue.
- [ ] Please send me the titles checked.

I enclose $_____ (No C.O.D.'s). All books
are 75c each. To help defray postage and handling
cost, please add 25c.

Name _____

Address _____

City/Town _____

State/Prov. _____ Zip _____

N 402